Sweet As
Sin

By: Britt Wolfe

First Edition: 2025
ISBN: 978-1-997664-04-8

Printed in Canada because books deserve a solid passport stamp too.

For inquiries, praise, declarations of undying love, or to request permission for use beyond fair dealing (seriously, just ask first), please visit: BrittWolfe.com

If you enjoyed this book, please consider leaving a review. If you didn't, well, that's between you and your questionable taste.

This novella is dedicated to:

Taylor—whose lyrics taught me that love can be both a prayer and a curse, both sanctuary and sin. Thank you for writing about women in their fullness: the tender and the furious, the faithful and the feral, the ones who love too much and the ones who learn to love themselves instead.

And for every woman who's ever written about love and darkness in the same breath.

For every voice that refused to choose between softness and strength, devotion and destruction, desire and survival.

Because you remind the world that women are never one thing— we are the whole story.

Sweet as Sin
Is Inspired by: *Don't Blame Me*
by Taylor Swift

This novella was born from *Don't Blame Me*, one of the most haunting songs on *Reputation*—a track that, to me, isn't really about falling in love at all, but about losing yourself inside it. It's about the kind of passion that burns straight through reason, where devotion becomes doctrine and love turns into its own dangerous form of faith. That's where this story began: with the idea that sometimes the most intoxicating kind of love isn't pure at all—it's poisonous, and we drink it anyway because we like the way it makes us feel.

Don't Blame Me was chosen by readers through a fan vote, where it went head-to-head against *Getaway Car*—and though I'm still a little heartbroken that *Getaway Car* didn't get to speed into the light just yet, it feels right that this was the one to win. *Don't Blame Me* isn't about escape. It's about surrender. About love so consuming it blurs the line between sinner and saint, salvation and destruction.

This story is for anyone who's ever loved like worship, who's ever mistaken obsession for connection, or faith for forgiveness—and who's learned, sometimes too late, that there's a fine line between devotion and ruin.

Because some loves don't just change you. They claim you.

Peace, love, and inspiration,

Britt Wolfe

Prologue ~ Melody's 16ᵗʰ Birthday

The house was the colour of sleep at that hour—everything blue-edged and gentle, as though the night had taken a last, soft breath and forgotten to exhale. In the kitchen, a single lamp cast a warm cone over the island, making a golden country of flour dust and ribbon trimmings. The oven hummed, reliable as a heartbeat. Cinnamon buns rose in their pan in the kind of slow-motion miracle that always felt a little like prayer—dough remembering what it had been, deciding what it wanted to become.

Valerie Meyers pressed the tail of a pink satin ribbon into a loop and pulled it through. The bow cinched perfectly, fat and jaunty on the corner of a box she'd wrapped at 3:17 a.m. when fatigue had blurred the edges of the world and made her giddy. A silver six and a gold one lay side by side on the island like two notes waiting for a melody. Sweet sixteen. Melody's sixteen. The thought ran through her like a spark.

"Okay," she whispered to no one and to the whole house at once. "Okay."

She was forty-three and had never learned how to make celebrations small. The kitchen bore witness: cellophane crackle, confetti sprinkles like sugared stars, a half-inflated balloon sagging away from its peers as if embarrassed by its own early failure to float. She had anchored the bouquet of pink and gold balloons to a mason jar of rice and tied it with a twine bow because the Pinterest tutorial had promised "rustic charm." The banner over the dining room entryway had fought her, curling at the ends, tape refusing to cling to eggshell paint. She'd finally used pushpins, driving them in with the heel of her hand, the letters wobbling slightly as if dancing: *Happy Sweet 16, Melody!*

She could have used a ladder. She could have woken Leo. But there was a holiness to doing it alone, the way mothers do, the way her own mother had once done with a stubbornness that lived on in Valerie like an heirloom. The work made the day real. It held back everything else—the bills they were a month late on, the faraway look in Leo's eyes lately, the way Max had started closing his door when he never used to, the new sharpness that sometimes flashed across Melody's face and vanished before Valerie could name it.

She placed the wrapped box—soft sweater, the one Melody had pointed to in the shop window and then pretended she didn't want—next to the cake stand. The cake itself waited in the fridge, frosted last evening in a smooth pale pink that had taken three tries and an embarrassing amount of swearing to achieve. She had piped sixteen tiny gold dots in a ring at the edge. It pleased her beyond reason.

The timer on the oven blinked from one minute to the next. She could hear the house around it—the refrigerator's intermittent mutter, the low snore from the family dog in the next room, the whispering of the thermostat as it debated whether to rouse the furnace. Beyond the glass of the back door, the yard lay in a skim of dew, grass silvered, the fence line a graphite sketch against the almost-morning.

Reading did pre-dawn like a secret. You could believe, in those blue hours, that the world might still be mended if you moved gently enough. Soon the bakery trucks would growl to life in the city centre, and the first shift would turn their collars up against the dark as they waited for buses. For now, it was just the old house and her, the soft weight of the day-to-be nestled in the curve of her ribs.

She checked the time—4:31—and smiled at her own ridiculousness. She'd slept hardly at all, dozing for twenty minutes at a time on the couch, waking with the conviction she'd forgotten the candles, the plates, the card. They were all there, of course, arranged in a satisfying fan: napkins scalloped in gold, paper plates with a blush of watercolour, candles thin and elegant as tapers. She had written in the card three times, a different tenderness each attempt, until she'd landed on something simple, something true: You changed the shape of my life the day you arrived. *Thank you for letting me be your mother. Love, Mom.*

She lifted the cinnamon buns from the oven and the room became a bakery: sugar and butter and the warm, cautious happiness of yeast. Steam threaded upward like silk. She brushed cream cheese icing across the soft spirals and watched it melt, sink, settle into the architecture of each coil. This—this was the reason she woke while the world slept. Not because the buns were necessary for a birthday, though they were, but because tending to something that transformed with attention felt like a way to show her love for the girl who first made her a mother.

Headlights skimmed the front windows.

They moved across the living room wall in a wash of pale, faltering light, not the neighbour's usual commute, not the stoic glide of the paper delivery. A second wash, angled higher. A door closed, firm. Another. Valerie froze, a ribbon loose in her hand.

Her first thought was delivery. She had ordered nothing. Her second was Leo—had he left something in the car when he came home from the late shift? No. The sedan had settled in the driveway with its particular sigh just after midnight, and he had come in smelling like crackers and stale coffee, kissed her hair, and been asleep almost before the sheets remembered the shape of him. The third thought was an older one, from childhood: have we done something wrong? It was ridiculous and still it came.

The knock was not a neighbour's knock. It was decisive, measured, the kind of sound that arrives with its own authority.

Every cell in Valerie's body said don't open the door. The older, practical part of her—the part that filed tax returns on time and knew where the passports were—said there is no reason not to. The knock came again, not louder, not urgent, but possessing. She wiped her hands on a tea towel and moved toward the front hall, feeling at once too slow and far too quick.

She opened the door to a porch full of uniforms.

Three marked cars idled at angles that blocked the street. An unmarked sedan crouched at the curb like a patient animal. The air was cold enough to turn their breath into ghosts. The porch light made pale rectangles of their faces and glossed the shoulders of their jackets. Two plainclothes detectives stood in front—woman on the left, man on the right—flanked by three uniformed officers; a fourth person, lean and watchful, hovered at the walkway with a camera cradled to their chest.

"Mrs. Meyers?" the female detective asked. Her voice was level, pitched to calm. She held something in her hand—folded papers that already carried the weight of what they would mean.

"Yes," Valerie said, and in the instant the word left her mouth she wished she could reach out and catch it, tuck it behind her teeth. "What—?"

"I'm Detective Alvarez. This is Detective Pritchard." A nod to the man at her side. He had a tired kindness about the eyes that seemed out of place here. "We have a warrant for the arrest of Melody Meyers."

The syllables landed like dropped plates. Valerie felt them shatter at her feet, scatter under furniture, hide themselves in places she wouldn't find until later.

"I—what?" She laughed, because her body did not know what else to do. It came out thin, bird-boned. "No. No, no. She's asleep. It's her birthday. She —what are you talking about?"

Detective Alvarez lifted the papers, reading formally, the way you read something you've read a hundred times but still understand will change the room. Name, date, judged signed, probable cause, charges—words that collected in the air like frost and made everything colder.

"We'll need to come in," Detective Pritchard said when she'd finished, voice gentle as if gentleness could make any of this less obscene. "We'll make this as straightforward as possible."

"Wait," Valerie said, still with her hand on the doorknob as if her grip could alter the shape of authority. "Wait, please. Just...what is this? You've made a mistake."

"We can't discuss details at this time," Alvarez said, and the words were a wall she knew she would bruise herself against. "We need to take Melody into custody. Where are your husband and your son?"

"My—Leo is asleep. Max..." Her eyes flicked toward the stairs of their own accord and found him there, small in the half-light, a boy in an oversized T-shirt with hair crushed to one side, his hand wrapped around the banister as if it were the only solid thing left in the world. He didn't speak. His eyes were enormous.

"Hey, buddy," Pritchard said softly, as if they'd come to change a tire. "Why don't you stay where you are for a minute."

A uniformed officer's radio crackled like static from another planet. Somewhere to the left, the photographer adjusted their strap. Valerie became aware, in a distant way, of the bare soles of her feet on the cool tile, the faint, impossible sweetness of icing and cinnamon that had become a kind of cruelty in the space of thirty seconds.

"Please," she said, because the word had been useful all her life. "Please. Just tell me—"

"We'll explain what we can as we move forward," Alvarez said. "Mrs. Meyers, I need you to step aside."

"I want to call a lawyer." The sentence arrived from some responsible part of her, a lighthouse flash in fog. "You can't—she's a child."

"She's sixteen," Pritchard said. "For the purposes of—" He stopped, rephrased. "We'll make sure her rights are protected."

"Her rights," Valerie repeated, and the phrase was unbearable.

Leo appeared in the doorway to the hall, lacing his belt as if he had come to fix something knocked out of place in the night. He blinked against the light, took in the police on the porch, the set of his wife's shoulders, the quiet wreck of his son on the stairs. He looked older than he had yesterday. He looked like a man who had not expected the morning to require him.

"What—?" he started, and then the room told him. "Mel?"

"We have a warrant," Alvarez said. "We're going to go upstairs now."

"Wait," Valerie said again, but it was softer and they were already moving, the way tide moves—inevitable, indifferent to sandcastles.

She went ahead of them because she didn't know how not to. She went on bare feet because she had always gone on bare feet in this house when something needed doing in the night. She felt the officers' presence behind her like a pressure change. The stairs announced them with their familiar complaint—third from the top, a long creak that always gave Max away when he tried to sneak a snack after bedtime.

At the top of the stairs she turned right without looking. She could have found her daughter's door with her eyes closed. It had the sticker she'd once thought was cute and now found irritating but never took down: a little vinyl sliver of a crescent moon with a face, as if the moon needed a personality. There was a chipped place in the white paint from the year they moved in, when a dresser had nudged the wall. She had not yet fixed it. The imperfection felt human. She wanted it to stay.

She knocked once, automatically, the way you knock on a door knowing the person inside is yours. Then she opened it.

Melody slept on her stomach, one hand crooked under her cheek, hair spilled like dark water across the pillow. It knocked the air out of Valerie to see her unafraid of the world, open-mouthed the way she'd slept when she was small. The room smelled faintly of the coconut shampoo she'd favoured lately and the spearmint gum she chewed to cover the smell of something else that Melody thought her mother didn't know about. A string of fairy lights—a summer's whim—hung across the bulletin board; a handful of Polaroids were pinned there in an unruly constellation: friends with their tongues sticking out, a boy with a shy face and lashes too long for fairness, a picture of Valerie and Melody at the fair last fall, faces pressed together, both laughing so hard their eyes were closed.

"Mel," Valerie said, a voice she tried to make ordinary. "Baby, wake up."

The detectives had entered behind her with a competence that made the word baby feel like something she should apologise for. A female uniformed officer—short, compact, with kind eyes that Valerie could not bear—stood just to the left of the doorway. Another officer had taken a place near the hall, angled so he could see the stairs.

"What's—" Melody pushed herself up on her forearms, sleep breaking off her like frost shaken from a branch. At first her expression was the endearing crankiness of a teenager woken too early. Then she saw the silhouettes behind her mother and everything in her face rearranged. "Mom?"

"It's okay," Valerie lied, because sometimes lies were the only bandage at hand. "It's—just listen." She turned to Alvarez. "Tell her everything you're going to do, and then tell her what to do to make it stop."

The words surprised her with their clarity. They surprised something in Alvarez too; the detective's eyes flicked to Valerie's, a brief acknowledgement that said: you are here, you are lucid, and I see it.

"Melody," Alvarez said, stepping forward enough to be seen but not enough to crowd the room. "I'm Detective Alvarez. This is Detective Pritchard. We have a warrant for your arrest."

"What?" Melody's voice did what Valerie's had refused to—jumped an octave, skittered across the rug. "For what?"

"I can't discuss details," Alvarez said, the formal cadence softened as much as it could be without becoming something else. "But I am going to advise you of your rights. You have the right to remain silent. You have the right to an attorney. If you cannot afford one—"

"I can," Valerie said reflexively, though she didn't know how she'd get the money. "We can."

"—one will be provided to you." Alvarez finished gently. "Do you understand these rights as I've explained them to you?"

"I didn't do anything," Melody said. The sentence arrived in a rush, bright with panic. She looked at her mother, not at the detectives. "Mom, I didn't —"

"Don't say anything," Valerie heard herself say, and the steadiness of her own voice startled her. "Not a word, darling. Not until a lawyer is here."

"I didn't—" Melody tried again, and the female officer stepped close enough to catch the next sentence before it could become a lifetime.

"Sweetheart," she said in a voice that had belonged to other girls in other rooms at other tender, terrible hours. "Your mom's right. Let her handle this part, okay?"

"Can I—" Melody's eyes flicked to the chair where her hoodie hung, the old navy one she loved, cuffs mangled. "Please?"

"Let's get you dressed," the officer said. She glanced at Alvarez, received a micro-nod, and turned to Valerie. "We'll give you a minute with her to change. I'll stay in the doorway."

Humiliation moved through the room like a weather front. Valerie could taste it. It tasted like metal.

She closed the door to a fingertip's width and put her hands on her daughter's shoulders. It felt like the wrong thing to do, and also like the only possible thing. Melody's skin was warm where the sheet had held it, her collarbone bird-delicate under the thin strap of a tank top. "Okay," Valerie said, and found a smile, the kind that had steadied skinned knees and first-day-of-school fretfulness and the night the upstairs window had rattled in a storm. "We're going to put on your warmest things. It's cold."

"I didn't do anything," Melody whispered, but now it had become an incantation, and Valerie couldn't tell whether it was to convince her or herself. Valerie pulled the hoodie over her daughter's head with the familiar, fussy tenderness of a thousand mornings, tugged the sleeves so the tattered cuffs swallowed her wrists. She helped her into jeans, socks, shoes. She wanted to brush her daughter's hair. She wanted, absurdly, to dab concealer under her eyes. She wanted every possible armour.

When she opened the door again, Alvarez nodded once. The female officer stepped forward with a pair of handcuffs held discreetly low.

"No," Valerie said, and then, because she needed to be the version of herself the room might listen to: "Is that necessary?"

"It is," Alvarez said. "We'll be respectful."

"Please," Valerie said, throat constricting. "Please, she's—she's sixteen."

The cuffs were silver and indifferent. The sound they made—metal kissing metal—was a small, obscene punctuation. Melody's face crumpled, steadied, smoothed. Valerie watched it happen—the move from a child's fear to the fierce, brittle composure of a person who will not give the room a spectacle. Pride and grief surged through her like the same tide.

"Mom," Melody said, voice shaking as she held out her hands. "Don't let them—"

"Shh," Valerie said, and touched her cheek. "Look at me." She did. In her eyes was everything—babyhood, braces, the first time she'd gone off the high diving board, the time she'd stormed out because Valerie had not let her go to a party where the mother was never home. There was also something else, something Valerie could not yet fully understand and would be afraid of when she could.

They walked. That was the word Valerie would land on later; there were so many ways to describe what happened, and she would choose "we walked." It gave her back a small part of the agency the moment had stolen. The hallway had never seemed so narrow. The family photos drew near and fell away like frames in a film—Max at three with a popsicle grin, Melody at ten with a science fair ribbon, the four of them at Cape May with sunburnt noses and enemy gulls in the background. The officers had done this before; they moved as if they had been measured for this space.

At the stairs, the female officer paused and turned to Melody. "We're going to take this one step at a time," she said, and the sentence might have been a kindness or nothing at all.

The descent stretched. On the fourth step from the bottom, the long creak announced them; Max flinched. Leo stood at the foot of the stairs, his hands half lifted and then useless against what they could not touch. He had always been good at heavy lifting, appliances muscled into place, trees dug out by the root. This was a different shape of weight.

"Mel," he said. The syllable came out strangled.

"Dad," she said, and he swallowed a sound that wanted to be a sob and not give it the oxygen.

Pritchard moved ahead to open the door. The house's cold night air rushed in again, unfamiliar now, unkind. The blue light of the unmarked car's dashboard blinked. A neighbour's upstairs window glowed briefly and went dark; Reading woke early.

"Can I—" Valerie began, and then stopped because there were too many verbs: come, ride, help, hold, fix.

"You can follow us to the station," Alvarez said. She had a way of placing words as if arranging fragile things on a shelf. "Don't bring any weapons. Don't bring—" She stopped, amended. "Just drive safe."

"Her phone," Valerie said. "Can she—?"

"We'll take her phone now," Alvarez said. "Personal items will be inventoried at intake."

The female officer guided Melody through the doorway, the hand at her elbow firm and not unkind. Outside, the air made Melody's breath a ghost too. She blinked against it, the way you blink against a wind that keeps finding the softest parts of the face.

"Mom," Melody said again, and that was the one that did it. Valerie's composure broke like thin ice. She moved forward, and the female officer stepped aside just enough, reading the room with a professional's instinct. Valerie put her hands on her daughter's face, pressed her forehead to hers as she had when Melody was a feverish toddler and only the cool of her mother's skin would persuade the heat to relent.

"I'm right behind you," Valerie said. The promise rang false and true at once. "Say nothing. We'll get a lawyer. We'll fix this."

"I didn't—" Melody started, and Valerie closed her eyes, because to hear the sentence would be to drag it up into the light where it could be examined by strangers.

They put her in the back of the unmarked car. The door thunked shut in a way that felt personal. The vehicles pulled away with the caution of people who understood that the dark contained sleeping neighbours and skateboard-abandoned helmets and cats who made foolish choices about wheels. In the hush after engines, the house made its familiar sounds again as if to prove it had not been a dream. The porch light hummed. Somewhere down the block, a sprinkler stuttered into life and corrected itself. A bird, disgusted with the whole business of human drama, tried out a tentative note and then thought better of it.

Inside, time did the thing it does in shock—it got thick, like honey left in the cold. Valerie found herself standing in the kitchen without remembering the steps it took to get there. The oven hummed because she had left it on. The cinnamon buns sat on the stove, icing glossy, cooling into a sweetness that now felt obscene. One of the balloons had given up and sagged low enough to bump the corner of the island each time the furnace exhaled; the sound was a small, repeated apology.

She picked up her phone and discovered she could not feel her fingers. She tapped in the contact for a lawyer she knew not at all, the name recommended long ago in a PTA Facebook thread she'd never believed she'd need. The screen blurred. She pressed call. Voicemail. She hung up and called again. She left a message that was a miracle of coherence. She did it again. She googled "Reading criminal defense" and took screenshots because her hands would not decide which to press. She looked up the number for the station. She did not call it. She would not give them her voice. She would only bring them her daughter and every ounce of fierce, practical love she could ballast in the trunk of the Honda.

Behind her, a chair scraped. Leo sat at the island and put his head in his hands. He had shaved last night and the shadow coming in already made him look bruised. In the doorway to the hall, Max stood like a question mark, the kind that ends a sentence you thought you knew.

Valerie lowered the phone and realised her other hand was clenched around a paper party horn, gold-foiled, ridiculous. She set it down as if it were evidence.

"What do we do?" Leo whispered.

The banner over the dining room entryway had lost one of its pushpins. "Happy Sweet 16, Melody!" slouched, the Y of "Happy" sagging low, a smile gone lopsided. The kitchen smelled of sugar and celebration and something else now—ozone from the open door, the metal tang of fear, a faint ghost of the cold the officers had carried in with them and left behind.

Valerie looked at the banner, at the icing glossing into a skin, at her son's small mouth gone white around the edges. She felt the shape of the day change under her feet. It tilted, and she found her grip.

"We start the car," she said, and did not recognise her own voice for a moment. It was steady as a measuring cup pressed flat against the counter to read the meniscus of milk. "We get dressed. We go."

She moved. She would move all day. She would move until there was nothing left to move and then she would find something else. The oven light glowed, stalwart. The furnace sighed. The banner breathed in and out in the gentle convection of the house.

"What do we do?" Leo said again, quieter, as if hoping the rightness of the words themselves might conjure an answer.

Valerie reached for her keys. Outside, the morning finally exhaled. The sky abandoned its blue grief and began, tentatively, to consider grey.

Part I
Before the Fall

The Golden Girl ~ Before

The August sun had a way of touching everything in Reading, Pennsylvania, as if the town were made of honey.

It dripped down over the red-brick houses, the narrow sidewalks, the white fences in need of new paint, until even the smallest imperfection looked blessed by light. On mornings like this, you could almost believe that beauty was proof of goodness, that golden things stayed that way.

Melody Meyers believed it—at least, she wanted to.

She stood at the bathroom mirror, the pale morning light turning her hair to burnished wheat. Her mother always said she'd been born with the right kind of hair, thick and dark, but brighter in the sun. She twisted a strand around her finger and let it fall. Sixteen was less than a year away, but she already looked older in this light. She smiled, then checked the angle of the smile. Too sweet? Too knowing? She tilted it a little until it seemed effortless.

There. Perfect again.

Downstairs, the kettle shrieked. The smell of toast carried up the stairs, rich with butter and cinnamon—her mother's weekday ritual, as dependable as prayer.

"Mel! You'll miss the bus!" Valerie called.

"I'm coming!" Melody grabbed her backpack, still open on her bed, and slid in a notebook, her planner, a tube of clear gloss. She left the zipper half undone. A calculated imperfection. It made her seem more human.

The Meyers' house sat on a street where all the mailboxes leaned slightly to one side, as if exhausted from years of bad news. The neighbours mowed their lawns on Saturdays and waved from driveways in ways that looked both friendly and performative. Everyone knew everyone—or thought they did.

Melody stepped out into the morning, sunlight spilling like applause. Across the street, Mrs. Harris watered her hanging baskets. The smell of wet petunias mingled with exhaust from a passing school bus.

"Morning, sweetheart!" the woman called.

"Morning!" Melody chirped, her voice light enough to float.

By the time she reached the bus stop, she was already aware of the eyes that followed her—boys in trucks, girls in clusters pretending not to look, a teacher leaning against his car with coffee steaming between his hands. She didn't resent it. She needed it. She'd learned young that attention was currency, and she was rich.

At school, everything gleamed. The halls smelled faintly of disinfectant and ambition. Lockers slammed in percussion. Melody moved through it all like a melody herself—notes placed just so, laughter spilling on cue.

Teachers adored her. She turned in essays that read like confessions and volunteered for every committee. She sang solos in choir with her eyes closed just long enough to seem genuine.

"Beautiful as always, Mel," said Mrs. Carter as the bell rang for third period. "You have such presence."

Melody smiled with practiced humility. "Thank you."

Presence. The word stuck. It made her think of something hovering—half-visible, almost holy.

But inside, she felt the opposite of holy. Inside was static. Restless static. She could ace every test, win every audition, and still feel the hollow hum underneath. Some nights she'd lie awake and picture herself peeling her skin off, not out of horror but curiosity—just to see what was underneath the good girl people worshipped.

At lunch, she sat with the same circle as always: Julia and Brooke and Hayley, the triumvirate of perfectly planned futures. They talked about colleges, about who was dating who, about how Coach Cal looked better this semester because he'd "finally stopped trying to be relatable."

Melody laughed at the right moments. She was good at that. But her eyes kept drifting toward the back of the cafeteria—to a table by the vending machines where the air seemed to hum differently.

Nick Halpern sat there, long-limbed, messy-haired, a scrawl of ink on his right hand from a pen that always seemed to explode. He wore the same navy jacket every day, sleeves pushed up, collar frayed. There was something about him that looked unfinished, like a sketch someone couldn't bear to complete.

"Who are you staring at?" Julia followed her gaze. "Oh God, Mel, not him."

Melody shrugged. "He's interesting."

"He's weird. He skipped homecoming last year to go to a concert in Philly. Alone."

Melody smiled faintly. "Maybe he just didn't like the music here."

Julia rolled her eyes, returning to her salad. But Melody kept looking. Nick had that particular stillness of people who lived mostly in their own heads. Every now and then, he would glance up as if sensing her gaze, and the air around her ribs would change pressure.

Later, when she thought back on it, she'd remember that moment as the first shift—the first crack in the glass of her carefully built world.

*　　*　　*　　*　　*

She met Nick again two days later in the library, where the light always looked older than the rest of the school. Dust floated like pollen in the shafts of sun from the high windows. Melody came for quiet and stayed for the feeling of being slightly outside of time.

Nick sat on the floor between shelves, a notebook open across his knees, pen dragging fast and furious. His backpack slouched beside him, leaking papers. She didn't mean to stop; she just did.

"What are you writing?" she asked.

He looked up. His eyes were a peculiar grey-green, like a storm thinking about happening. "A song."

"Oh." She blinked. "You're a musician."

He shrugged. "I try."

"Can I see?"

He hesitated, then turned the notebook around. The lyrics were raw, sharp. Lines crossed out, rewritten, circled. Words about drowning and devotion and something that might have been love if it hadn't sounded so dangerous.

"It's beautiful," she said.

"It's messy."

"So is everything worth feeling."

He smiled a little at that—quick, private—and she felt something shift inside her, the way floorboards settle under new weight.

They started talking after that. About music mostly, but also about the kind of things that felt too big for Reading: infinity, faith, death, why people pretended to be okay when they weren't. He said he liked the way her mind worked.

She said he saw things no one else did.

When he told her he'd never met anyone like her, she believed him. When he said she made the world make sense, she didn't know it yet, but she believed that too.

*   *   *   *   *

They began to meet everywhere and nowhere: under the bleachers after choir practice, in the narrow alley behind the old theatre where the brick still smelled of rain, in his car on the edge of town where the radio static was louder than the music.

He called her *Melody*, always in full, never Mel. He said shortening it would be a sin—something about how names carried spells. She laughed then, but sometimes she caught herself whispering his name before sleep, as if it could conjure him.

She started wearing his jacket, too big and too warm, the cuffs swallowing her hands. Her mother noticed.

"New coat?" Valerie asked one evening over dinner, her tone bright but cautious.

"Just borrowed," Melody said. She didn't look up.

Leo grinned. "Secret boyfriend?"

Max giggled.

Melody rolled her eyes, but her pulse jumped. "Dad."

Valerie smiled, but there was something thoughtful behind it, a note slightly off key. "Just be careful, honey. First loves can feel like fireworks, but fireworks don't last."

Melody stabbed at her peas. "Maybe I'm not afraid of burning."

*   *   *   *   *

Autumn came early that year, sharp and merciless. The air smelled of leaves and distant fires. Every afternoon, the sun leaned low and gold over the football field, catching in the brass of the marching band's horns.

It was on one of those afternoons that Nick kissed her for the first time.

They were sitting on the hood of his car at the edge of the quarry, feet tangled, the air humming with late-day insects. The water below them reflected the sky in impossible shades of amber and blue.

"I don't know what this is," he said, voice quiet but unsteady.

"What, what is?"

"This." He gestured between them. "You. Me. It feels like—like I swallowed lightning."

Her laugh caught somewhere in her throat. "Then don't spit it out."

He looked at her for a long moment, and she felt stripped bare—not undressed, but seen. Then he leaned forward and kissed her. It wasn't tentative. It wasn't sweet. It was consuming. And she let it take over all of her.

The world telescoped: light, breath, heartbeat. Every cell in her body rearranged around his touch. When they pulled apart, the air felt wrong without him. She wanted him again. And again.

Nick pressed his forehead against hers. "I think you'll ruin me."

She smiled. "Maybe I already have."

Later, she'd remember that too—the way he'd said it with awe, not fear. The way she'd felt something uncoil inside her, something that had waited years to be fed.

They became inseparable. Every hallway glance, every shared cigarette behind the gym, every midnight text was another thread in the web she spun around them.

Nick started missing classes. He said he couldn't concentrate, that she'd scrambled his brain. She loved it. The power of it.

When he played his guitar, she'd sit so close she could feel the vibration through her ribs. When he wrote songs about her, she copied the lyrics into her notebook, her own handwriting binding them to her.

In the beginning, it felt like worship. Later, it would feel like ownership. But that came slowly, so slowly she mistook it for love.

*   *   *   *   *

By winter, the town was shrouded in frost. Streetlights turned halos in the cold. They drove through it all—windows cracked, music up, her hair whipping around her face. She tasted metal and freedom and something sweeter.

She began skipping choir practice. Stopped answering her friends' texts. Her grades slipped a little, not enough to alarm, just enough to notice.

When Nick said she was the only real thing he'd ever known, she pressed her hand to his chest and promised him the same.

The world shrank to the size of them, and she thought it was enough.

But sometimes, late at night, she'd catch her reflection in the dark window and not recognize herself. There was a gleam in her eyes that didn't look like joy. It looked like hunger.

She told herself it was what love did—it hollowed you out so you could hold more of the other person. She didn't yet understand how dangerous that kind of devotion could become.

*   *   *   *   *

On a crisp night, she and Nick parked on the hill above the river. The town glittered below them—tiny, fragile, oblivious.

He turned down the radio. The silence was intimate, heavy.

"What are you thinking?" he asked.

She watched the lights blur through the windshield. "That I never want it to change."

"It won't," he said. "I promise."

She turned to him then, searching his face, memorizing it. "You can't promise that."

"I can," he said, and kissed her again, and for a moment she believed him. The wind pressed against the car windows. Far off, a train wailed through the dark—a long, mournful note that sounded almost like warning. Melody closed her eyes and thought, If the world ever tries to take this from me, I'll burn it down.

She didn't mean it. Not yet. But somewhere deep inside, the spark heard her.

And it waited.

The snow in Reading never lasted long. It came soft and secret, turning the world to lace for a few hours before melting back into the dirt and the gutters. The city couldn't hold beauty for long—it always dissolved. Melody told herself she liked that about it, that impermanence kept things pure. But when she said it, she thought of Nick, and her stomach ached in a way that felt nothing like purity.

They'd been together a few weeks now. Not officially—not in the way her friends asked about—but real enough that she carried him with her everywhere, a pulse beneath her ribs. Every text, every glance, every stolen hour in his car was another breath she didn't know how to live without. She could still taste the quarry on her tongue—the iron edge of the air, the sweetness of being chosen.

But love, she was learning, didn't stop the rest of the world from intruding.

Her grades had slipped. Not badly, but enough for her father to notice. Enough for her mother to suggest, gently, that she might "benefit from a little academic support." Melody had laughed it off, promised she'd catch up, but Valerie had already called the university's tutoring centre.

"She's Swedish," her mother said that morning over oatmeal. "An exchange student at Alvernia. Charlotte Nilsson. She tutors in calculus and physics, apparently brilliant."

Melody's spoon froze mid-air. "Swedish?"

Valerie smiled. "Don't sound so suspicious. She's older, twenty maybe. It'll just be once or twice a week until you're back on track."

"I am on track."

"I know, sweetheart. But it's not a punishment. Think of it as help."

Leo rustled the newspaper. "I think it's a good idea. A little extra help never hurt anyone."

Melody wanted to say I don't need her, but the look on her mother's face stopped her. The pride there was fragile, a glass bauble she couldn't bear to drop. So she nodded and took another spoonful, tasting nothing.

Charlotte arrived on a Thursday afternoon smelling of snow and eucalyptus.

She was the kind of beautiful that made rooms go still for a beat—the tall, fair kind that seemed effortless. Her hair was the palest gold, her eyes so light they almost looked translucent. When she smiled, her teeth were the exact shade of porcelain coffee cups.

"Hello," she said, accent soft but distinct, the vowels rounded like river stones. "You must be Melody."

The voice alone felt like a warning.

Melody nodded, taking in the wool coat, the sleek leather boots, the small silver cross at her throat. She wanted to hate her instantly, but Charlotte disarmed hatred by being kind. Infuriatingly kind.

"I've heard so much about you," Valerie said, beaming. "You're exactly what Melody needs. Coffee? Tea?"

"Tea, please. If it's no trouble."

The two of them moved easily into conversation—the mother and the miracle tutor—while Melody watched, polite and wordless. Charlotte's every gesture was practiced grace: the way she set her gloves on the table, the way she tucked her hair behind one ear, the faint musicality of her laughter.

She looked like she belonged in another country entirely, somewhere cleaner, calmer, where people never raised their voices. The kind of place Melody used to dream about escaping to before she realized escape only mattered if someone was chasing you.

They began with derivatives. Charlotte's handwriting was precise, almost architectural. She explained things in a low, melodic tone that made the numbers sound like a hymn. Melody nodded, followed along, and hated that she understood it better than she had all semester.

"You're quick," Charlotte said, smiling. "You only need someone to remind you that you are."

The compliment should have warmed her. Instead it prickled.
She wanted to say *I don't need reminding.*
She wanted to say *I already have someone who believes in me.*

But she didn't. She smiled back and watched the woman's pale fingers tap lightly on the page as she spoke.

Nick came to pick her up later that afternoon, headlights cutting through the early dusk. The sound of his engine had become its own kind of music to her—familiar, thrilling, the world rearranging itself to make space for him.

Charlotte was gathering her notes when the knock sounded. Valerie called from the kitchen, "That'll be Nick!"

"Nick?" Charlotte repeated, curiosity softening her features. "Your boyfriend?"

Melody hesitated, then nodded. "Yeah. He plays guitar."

The word felt both defiant and dangerous.

Charlotte's smile didn't falter, but something passed through her expression—quick as a shadow across water. "How sweet. First love, yes?"

Before Melody could respond, Nick stepped into the doorway. He looked tired, hair damp from melting snow, jacket collar turned up. His presence filled the room like static.

"Hey, Mel," he said. Then he saw Charlotte.

It was barely a moment—a flicker, a glance—but Melody saw it happen. The way his eyes lingered half a second too long. The small, almost imperceptible shift in his posture. Charlotte smiled at him politely, nothing more. But the air between them thickened.

"Nick, this is Charlotte," Valerie said brightly. "Melody's tutor."

"Nice to meet you," he said, offering his hand. She took it. Their fingers touched. It was nothing. It was everything.

"Likewise," Charlotte said. "You're a musician?"

Nick blinked. "Uh—yeah."

"You must show me sometime. I love music."

Melody's stomach twisted, a slow coil of something she didn't fully understand. She laughed too loudly. "We should go, Mom. Traffic."

Valerie waved, oblivious. "Drive safe, you two!"

In the car, silence hung heavy. The heater blew warm air against the windows, fogging the glass. Melody stared straight ahead, fingers drumming against her knee.

"She seems nice," Nick said finally.

"Yeah. She's...fine."

"From Sweden, right? That accent's wild."

Melody's jaw tightened. "You think so?"

He glanced at her, confused by her tone. "What? I was just saying—"

"Forget it."

He sighed, turning up the radio. The hum of an old love song filled the car, syrupy and unbearable. She hated it. She loved it. She wanted to crawl inside the sound and never come out.

*　　*　　*　　*　　*

Charlotte became a fixture in the Meyers' house. Twice a week, then three. Sometimes she stayed for dinner if Valerie insisted, which she often did. "You're far from home," she'd say, ladling stew into bowls. "You shouldn't eat alone."

Charlotte always smiled, modest and grateful. "You're too kind."

Melody learned details she didn't want: Charlotte's hometown on the coast near Gothenburg, the brother who played cello, the scholarship that brought her here. She volunteered at a literacy centre. She took photos of clouds. She prayed before eating, eyes closed, lashes trembling like moth wings.

Everything about her was delicate. Effortless. Good.

And that was the problem.

Goodness made people trust you. Goodness made people love you without your permission.

Melody began to notice things—the way her father's voice softened when he spoke to Charlotte, the way her mother laughed more easily in her presence, the way Max lingered at the table when she told stories. Everyone fell under her spell.

Nick, she told herself, would never.

Still, the image of their handshake replayed in her mind at night, looping like a song she couldn't turn off. His eyes meeting hers. That quick, unreadable current between them.

She began to test him—small things at first.

Who are you texting?

What did you do after school?

You like girls like that, don't you—perfect ones.

He always laughed, kissed her forehead, told her she was crazy. She told herself he was right.

But the seed had already been planted.

One afternoon in late February, the air brittle with cold, Charlotte arrived wearing a pale blue sweater that made her look like she belonged in a snow globe. Melody had left her notebook upstairs, and when she came down, she found her mother and Charlotte talking quietly at the kitchen counter.

"She's been working so hard," Valerie said. "I just hope she isn't spreading herself too thin."

"She's bright," Charlotte replied. "Sometimes the bright ones need reminding they don't have to burn to be seen."

Melody froze in the doorway. The words felt invasive, like someone reading her diary aloud.

Charlotte looked up and smiled. "Ready to start?"

"Yeah," Melody said. The air between them felt sharp.

They worked through equations in silence. Charlotte's pencil glided across the paper with serene precision. When she leaned over to correct a line, Melody caught the faint scent of her perfume—something floral and old-fashioned. It made her dizzy.

Halfway through the session, Charlotte's phone buzzed. She glanced at it, smiled faintly, and turned it face down.

"Sorry," she said. "A friend."

Melody nodded, pretending not to care. But the shape of that smile burned into her mind.

Nick was waiting outside again. When he saw them through the window—Charlotte handing Melody her textbook, touching her arm lightly—his face softened. He waved. Charlotte waved back.

Something inside Melody splintered, invisible and immediate.

"See you next week," Charlotte said. "Don't forget to check the last proof—it's tricky."

"I won't," Melody said. Her voice sounded wrong in her own ears.

Charlotte slipped on her coat and stepped out into the twilight, her silhouette swallowed by snow. The door clicked shut.

Melody stood for a moment, watching the empty space she'd left behind. Then she grabbed her bag and stormed out to the car.

"Everything okay?" Nick asked as she slid into the seat.

"Fine."

"You sure?"

"I said I'm fine."

They drove in silence until the stoplight at Ninth Street. The red glow bled across his face, beautiful and unfamiliar.

Finally, she turned to him. "Do you think she's pretty?"

He blinked. "Who?"

"You know who."

"Charlotte? She's nice. That's all."

"That's not what I asked."

He frowned. "What's going on with you lately?"

"Nothing."

"You've been weird."

"I'm *fine*." The word cracked on the way out. She pressed her nails into her palm, the sting anchoring her. "I just—forget it."

He sighed, drumming his fingers on the wheel. "You've got to stop looking for ghosts, Melody."

She stared out the window. The streetlights blurred into streaks of gold. Somewhere behind her eyes, something began to hum—a low, relentless note she couldn't silence.

That night, Melody lay awake listening to the house breathe. Max's soft snore down the hall. The radiator ticking. The whisper of snow against the windowpane.

She replayed the afternoon in her mind—the glance, the wave, the way Charlotte's hair had caught the light. It was nothing. It was everything.

She tried to picture Nick's face when he looked at her, the warmth there, the softness. But the image kept flickering, Charlotte slipping into the frame, her smile too serene, too knowing.

Jealousy, she told herself, was ugly. Love wasn't jealous. Love was pure. But she'd never seen purity look like this before.

She turned on her side.

She thought about Charlotte's delicate hands, the way they'd brushed Nick's. She thought about the way goodness could hide something greedy underneath, something that took and took and still smiled politely.

She thought about fire—how beautiful it looked from a distance, how it could erase everything and still call it cleansing.

By dawn, she'd convinced herself she wasn't jealous at all.

She was only protecting what was hers.

Worship

By March the snow was gone, leaving the streets of Reading slick with thaw and the promise of something brighter that would never quite arrived. The gutters gurgled, the trees wept sap, and every surface smelled faintly of mud and rain. Melody felt the same way—damp around the edges, raw with wanting.

School blurred. Days lost their shape. She still moved through them, of course—smiling at teachers, exchanging notes with Brooke, singing when the choir director cued her—but everything outside of Nick felt like background noise. She could not remember what she'd cared about before him. She could barely remember herself.

Her notebooks had changed. Where once there had been equations and vocabulary lists, there were now fragments:
a line from a song he'd hummed,
a sketch of his hands wrapped around a guitar neck,
a sentence she couldn't stop rewriting—*the way he looks at me feels like absolution.*

The pages filled quickly, words pressing close as if trying to breathe the same air. Sometimes she signed his name beneath her own, testing how the letters looked together. Melody Halpern. She liked the symmetry. She liked the claim.

"Mel, are you listening?" Mrs. Carter's voice cut through the fog.

Melody blinked. The classroom had emptied except for a few students packing their bags. A test paper sat face-down on her desk, the red 78 circled twice.

"I'm sorry," she said. "I didn't sleep well."

Mrs. Carter sighed. "You're usually so focused. Is everything okay?"
"Fine."

"You've missed two assignments this week."

"I'll catch up."

Her teacher hesitated, then lowered her voice. "You know, first love can do that. It's wonderful—but don't let it take all the room in your life."

Melody smiled politely, already halfway out the door. Advice always sounded like envy.

At home her mother watched her the way people watch a candle burning too close to the drapes.

"You've been distracted," Valerie said one evening while they folded laundry. "Your teachers emailed again."

"I'm still passing."

"That's not the point. You've always cared about doing well."

"I still do."

Valerie smoothed a T-shirt over her knee. "I'm happy you're happy, honey. I just don't like the way you talk about him sometimes. 'Mine' isn't a word you use about people."

Melody looked up, heat rushing to her face. "You call Dad yours."

"That's different."

"How?"

Valerie opened her mouth, closed it again. "Because love isn't ownership. It's—"

Melody cut her off. "You wouldn't understand."

She carried her stack of clothes upstairs, every step louder than it needed to be. Behind her, she heard her mother's soft exhale—the sound of surrender disguised as patience.

Her room had become a shrine.

The walls were lined with Polaroids: Nick at the quarry, Nick's hand holding hers across the gearshift, the blurry silhouette of his face in the glow of a dashboard light. On her dresser, a dried wildflower he'd picked in October lay beneath a glass tumbler. His jacket hung over her chair, still faintly smelling of smoke and pine. She'd tried washing it once; the scent vanished and she'd cried until dawn.

Every night before bed she opened her journal. The pages had become confessionals.

He said he loved the way I looked when I'm angry. I think that means he loves all of me. If he ever left, the world would collapse inward. Maybe that's what black holes are—girls like me losing the thing they orbit.

Sometimes she drew small red hearts beside his name, but they never looked soft enough, so she shaded them darker until they turned almost black.

*   *   *   *   *

One night at dinner, Leo tried humour to bridge the quiet.

"Still seeing the young Romeo?" he asked, spooning potatoes onto his plate.

Melody smiled tightly. "Every day."

"Maybe take a day off, huh? Let the poor guy breathe," Leo tested out a smile as he passed the potatoes to Max.

"She's in love," Valerie said, though her tone was cautious. "Remember being that age?"

"Sure," Leo said. "But I don't remember skipping algebra for it."

"It's fine," Melody said. "I'm fine."

Valerie met Leo's eyes across the table, a wordless exchange that made Melody's chest tighten. She hated when they did that—talked in glances, as if she were a problem to be solved instead of a person.

Later she heard them downstairs, voices low.

"I don't like it," her mother was saying. "She's obsessed. The way she talks about him—'mine,' 'forever,' like she's casting a spell."

"She's fifteen," Leo replied. "It'll burn out."

"I'm not so sure."

Melody closed her door, heart hammering. She pressed her ear to the wood until their voices blurred into murmurs. Then she turned the lock and leaned against it, breathing hard.

They don't understand.

Love wasn't a spell. It was gravity. It pulled everything toward it until nothing else existed.

*   *   *   *   *

In April, choir rehearsals began for the spring concert. Melody was supposed to sing a solo—*Bridge Over Troubled Water*. But halfway through the first verse her voice broke. Mrs. Carter stopped playing, frowning.

"Again from the top."

Melody tried. The notes stuck in her throat. She could hear Nick's voice in her head instead, low and rough, the way he'd whispered to her the night before: You're the only thing keeping me sane.

After rehearsal, Mrs. Carter touched her shoulder. "You look pale. Go home and rest."

Rest. The word meant nothing anymore. Rest was what other people did, and something she didn't have time for.

She started walking to Nick's house after sunset, cutting through backyards where the grass was still damp from rain. His window glowed faintly at the top of the stairs. Sometimes he'd open it when she threw a pebble, grin down at her, whisper for her to climb up. Other nights the light stayed dark. She'd wait anyway, whispering his name like prayer beads: *Nick, Nick, Nick.*

When he finally appeared, rumpled and half-awake, she felt saved.

He'd laugh. "You're gonna get caught."

"Then catch me," she'd whisper.

They'd drive to the reservoir, sit on the hood of his car, watch the lights ripple on the water. He'd talk about music, about leaving Reading someday, about how nothing here ever changed. She'd nod, but in her mind she was screaming *Don't leave me here.*

He never heard it. Or maybe he did and thought it was the wind.

The more she loved him, the smaller the world became.

Her friends stopped texting. Charlotte had gone back to Sweden for spring break, but Melody still thought about her sometimes, how she'd smiled at Nick that afternoon, how his eyes had softened. She told herself it was nothing, yet the thought returned whenever Nick was late to reply.

She began to check his messages when he wasn't looking. Once she found a text from a classmate, Sarah, asking about a history assignment. Nothing more. Still, her hands shook as she deleted it.

She started wearing his jacket again, even when it was too warm. The weight of it steadied her, reminded her he was real. When other girls looked at him in the halls, she smiled politely but catalogued their faces, memorized the threat.

She wrote a list in her notebook one afternoon:

Things worth dying for:
1. Nick
2. Love
3. Nick again

She drew a heart beside it, then a small flame.

*   *   *   *   *

By May her mother had run out of gentle words.

"This isn't healthy," Valerie said one night. "You don't eat. You barely sleep. You've stopped talking to your friends."

"I talk to Nick," Melody had protested.

"That's not the same."

"It's better."

"Melody." Valerie's voice cracked. "Love shouldn't make you smaller."

Melody looked up from her notebook. "Maybe it's supposed to."

Her mother stared at her for a long time, then left the room quietly. The door closed with the sound of finality.

That night the house was asleep, the air thick with summer's first heat. Melody sat at her desk, the lamp throwing a golden halo around her journal. She wrote without thinking, hand cramped, words tumbling faster than she could read them.

You're the only real thing.
When we kiss, I disappear.
If love doesn't undo you, it's not real.

Ink smudged under her palm. She didn't care. The words weren't for keeping. They were for releasing—like smoke from a struck match.

She tore a page out, folded it, slipped it into the box where she kept the small relics of him: ticket stubs, guitar picks, the thread from his frayed cuff. Her heart beat so loudly she could hear it echo in the hollow places of the house.

Outside, the wind rattled the window. Somewhere a dog barked once, then fell silent.

Melody rose, crossed to the sill, and knelt.

The moon hung low and bruised above the neighbourhood, washing the rooftops in pale silver. She pressed her forehead to the glass. Her breath fogged it, then cleared.

She thought of church, of prayers half-learned as a child—knees on cold tile, her mother's hand guiding hers. But this wasn't for God. God had nothing to do with this. God was too small.

She whispered into the dark, voice trembling with reverence.

"Love, make me worthy of him. Make me holy in the way he looks at me."

The words felt alive, crawling through her veins like current. She closed her eyes.

"It's not my fault," she murmured, the phrase slipping out before she knew she'd thought it. "Nick makes me crazy. Love makes me crazy. It has to. That's how you know you're doing it right."

The house was silent except for her breathing. She stayed there for a long time, palms pressed together, moonlight on her face, waiting for an answer that would never come.

But something in the quiet answered anyway—soft, invisible, dangerous. It felt like a promise.

The Betrayal

By June, Reading smelt of cut grass and hot tar, the kind of heat that made the road shimmer as if the town were a mirage about to admit it had been pretending to be real. The school year staggered toward its end—the bulletin boards bleached by sun through classroom windows, mural paint peeling in thin curls, the final assemblies droning with congratulatory names. On paper, Melody Meyers was doing fine enough to pass through the gates; in the air around her, everything felt off by a degree or two, like a picture frame crooked just enough to become the only thing you could see in a room.

Nick had changed in ways you could miss if you didn't know him like a map. At first it was a missed call returned an hour late with a warm apology. Then it was two. Then a message that read, *Can't tonight—helping Ben with a project*, which should have been harmless but landed in her chest with a dull, recognizable thud.

When they were together, his hands still found hers in the dark. He still tucked a curl behind her ear with theatrical tenderness and grinned when she rolled her eyes. But sometimes, when he looked away, the space he left behind didn't fill back in right away. Melody noticed the lag. She started to count the seconds.

One night he cancelled with a softness that asked her not to be hurt. "I promised my mom I'd fix the porch light," he said, and she pictured him up a step ladder, jaw clenched in concentration, forearms shown off by the angle of the task—something sweetly domestic, something that made the future feel obedient. She said "Of course," because she had learned the performance of easy, but after dinner, with the neighbourhood sliding into lavender, she put on his too-warm jacket and walked the chalk-lined path between backyards to the street near his.

From there you could see the front of his house without being seen. She knew the pattern of it intimately: the splay of rose bushes along the steps, the porch swing that favoured the left, the upstairs rectangle of light that meant he was in his room, the downstairs lamp that meant his mother was reading with her feet tucked up under her.

Tonight, the upstairs window was dark. The porch was empty. The driveway—empty too. No car. No Nick trying to fix anything. The sinkhole that opened in her stomach was small and mean and immediately disorienting. She put a hand against the rough bark of the maple on the verge, the way you steady yourself when the ground pitches on a boat you didn't realize had left shore.

Maybe he'd gone to the hardware store. Maybe he'd run for takeout. Maybe, maybe. The possibilities multiplied like ants.

She walked home slowly, the jacket heavy as blame. When he called later, breathless and cheerful, she hated the sound of relief his voice pulled from her.

"Hey," he said, "sorry—Ben's place turned into a marathon. He's hopeless at history."

"You said porch light."

A half-beat. "Right—earlier. Then Ben called. I texted—did you not get it?" She looked down at her phone where there was, indeed, a message she hadn't seen, the preview banner wiped away by a notification about the weather and the nonsense of her own constantly refreshing mind. The proof didn't soothe the sore place. "I guess I missed it," she said. "How's the light?"

"Fixed. You okay, Mel?"

"I'm fine."

"I'll make it up to you tomorrow."

He said it like a promise and it slid into the part of her that collected promises like smooth stones. She should have been satisfied. Instead, even in the sweetness of his voice, she thought of Charlotte saying the word first love like a benediction and her stomach went tight with something that looked like superstition and felt like fury.

The tutoring had been tapering since early spring, but the day it ended felt like a door closing softly on a room still full of the people you loved. "I'm sorry," Charlotte said at the dining table, fingers folded neatly atop her notebook. "My summer term is busier than I expected. I don't want to do a poor job for you." She smiled in that way she had—quiet, reverent, as if the act of telling you bad news could be made graceful.

Valerie did her best to hide her disappointment. "You've been wonderful. We're so grateful you came into our lives."

We, Melody noted. As if Charlotte had done something more than teach derivatives and drink tea while the house re-arranged itself around her composure. Melody wanted to say, *You could stay if you wanted to. People make time for the things they want.* Instead, she smiled and told Charlotte she understood and tried to ignore the static under her skin.

"Before I go back home for the summer," Charlotte added, eyes bright with a faraway light. "It is better to focus."

Back home. The words should have been a charm. Instead they felt like a move in a game Melody hadn't learned the rules to.

The next afternoon, Melody took the bus downtown because the bus is good for thinking if you can ignore the lives you ride through: old women with grocery bags, a boy with a skateboard scuffed to bone, a couple arguing in whisper-shouts over a text message neither could unread. Reading's centre is a handful of blocks with the personality of a town that keeps telling you it's a city—café windows crowded with plants, a thrift shop with cowboy boots in its display, a record store that always smelt like pine cleaner and longing.

She walked into Crux Café because the air-conditioning there was ambitious, because the tabletops were mis-matched, because the barista never remembered anyone's name exactly but pretended he did with an intimacy that made you spend more than you meant to. The place was a greenhouse of people wishing to be seen. Melody ordered an iced latte and pretended to read. She was mid-pretence when the bell over the door tittered and let in a ribbon of heat and two silhouettes—the second one so instantly recognizable her whole body performed a small electric trick.

Nick. In his grey T-shirt that made every freckle on his arms look like punctuation, in that thoughtless way he moved through space as if the air was in love with him. And beside him—Charlotte, her hair pulled back, a white summer dress like a scold to everything that ever tried to stain it.

They didn't kiss. They didn't touch. They stood close enough that the conversation could layer itself without effort. Charlotte's laugh arrived and settled itself in the room like incense. Nick said something and the corner of her mouth tilted in that quiet, private way Melody had once decided was holiness and now read as hunger disguised as restraint.

For a moment, the café was a painting. The light fell just so; the plants in the window made green lace on Charlotte's skin; the condensation on Nick's glass tracked a wandering stream.

Melody set her cup down so carefully the ice didn't dare clink. She stood, slower than she meant to, and ghosted along the long shelf of zines and handbills at the back of the café, holding up a flyer as if the show it promised might save her life. She was near enough to hear Charlotte say "—really proud of the work you're doing—" and Nick answer with something like, "—You should see the new lyrics, they're—" and the rest a hush because the world chose that moment to let loose the espresso machine's shuddering gasp.

Intimacy doesn't require touch. It's a grammar. Melody heard the punctuation in their voices. She read the pause after his compliment. She saw the way Charlotte bent forward to listen, the way people do when what's across from them is precious.

For a shorn second, the world went incorporeal. It was the feeling you get when you misstep in the dark and your ankle turns. Then it returned, and with it, the loud, clinical fact of it: her beautiful boy sitting with the girl who had been welcomed into her house and her mother's good dishes and her father's easy jokes and who had now, quietly, decided to be busy with everything but this.

Melody left without finishing her drink. On the sidewalk, heat lifted off the pavement in waves. Two girls walked past arm in arm, laughing about a text, the skin of their shoulders pinked by sun. A man loaded crates of peaches onto a market table, the scent of them so generous it felt like an apology she hadn't been offered. She walked home in a straight line that wasn't at all straight, each storefront warping as she passed as if glass might choose to be water.

Nick called that night as if nothing in the universe had made any decision at all. "Hey," he said. "You around?"

"Where were you this afternoon?" she asked, voice even, polite, viciously tender.

A pause. "Practise. Why?"

"Crux Café have a rehearsal space now?"

The pause tightened. "You were there?"

"I was."

"It's not—Mel, it's not what you think."

"Then what is it?"

"A coffee. She wanted feedback on a grant application. She's—" His tone shifted, reflexively protective. "She's leaving at the end of the summer. She just wanted—"

"She just wanted," Melody repeated, and the phrase tasted like holding a blade by the sharp part. "She ended tutoring because she's too busy. With grant applications."

"That's not fair."

"Fair," she said softly. She repeated herself, testing the word for weaknesses. "You could have told me."

"I didn't think it mattered."

There. Not a confession, exactly, but a precise nick in the veneer. He rushed to correct it. "I mean, I didn't want you to get... upset."

"Because you think I'm the kind of girl who gets upset."

"I think you care too much."

There was a long quiet. She could hear his breath. She could hear her own, matched to his without permission like two metronomes finding the same beat in separate rooms. She pictured Charlotte's pale hands folded around a white cup, the condensation sliding down like a slow tear. She pictured the way Nick leaned in when he wanted to be better understood.

"Meet me," she said. "Now."

"Mel—" he began.

"It's not a request."

He exhaled, an old-man sound in a young mouth. "Fine. The field behind the school?"

"Twenty minutes."

She hung up before he could say her name like a caress and a tether.

Outside, the summer light had moved from gold to metal. She walked to the field with the tired determination of a person dragging a net through water, sure of the things it would pull up and sickened by the knowing. Crickets started up at the ditch edge as if her arrival had been rehearsed. Somewhere a sprinkler worked itself into a rhythm and then forgot it.

Nick arrived late by two minutes, hair pushed up by the heel of his hand, a tell she used to read as boyish and now read as strategy. He stood there, beautiful and careless, and she almost hated him for the audacity of having a face that stayed gentle even when his choices weren't.

"Hey," he said, wary-soft. "You look—"

"Please don't complete that sentence."

He laughed once, false, and looked down at his shoes. "Okay."

She stepped closer. "Were you with her yesterday too? When you cancelled—Ben's project?"

"No." His eyes lifted to hers, clear and open and marred by a microscopic flinch.

"You're lying."

"I'm not."

"You are."

"Mel—"

"Say you're lying," she said, and the way she said it made a bird startle out of the grass as if the air itself had been struck.

He rubbed the back of his neck, turning away. "You scare me sometimes."

The words fell between them like an unlit match. She was the one who bent to pick it up.

"Why?"

"Because you don't leave space for anything else. For me to be anything but yours every second of every day." He turned back. In the failing light, his face looked older, or perhaps just more tired. "You can't love someone so much you stop being yourself, Mel. That's not love. It's—" He caught himself. "It's too much."

The part of her that had felt holy at his touch flared into something else, a white, useless light. For a second, she could smell Crux Café—eucalyptus and espresso, Nick's laugh. She could see Charlotte's profile edged in window-fern. She could hear her own mother saying, *Mine' isn't a word you use about people.*

"Too much," she whispered, as if memorising a diagnosis. She stepped back and the field tilted.

He reached for her, palms open. "I'm not trying to hurt you."

"Then why does it feel like being peeled?" she asked. "Why does it feel like you've put me in a jar and you're holding me up to the light and saying, 'Look how pretty when contained.'"

"Melody—"

"That coffee, Nick," she said, voice going steadier than she felt. "Did you talk about me?"

"Of course."

"What did you say?"

"That you're brilliant and you make me better and that sometimes I don't know how to carry how much this is."

"'This' being me."

"This being *us*."

A wind came up from nowhere and pressed the field flat for a moment, every blade of grass bowing in the same direction, then lifting, confused, as if deciding together had been a mistake. She thought about prayer, the kneeling, the vow whispered against the glass. She thought about promises made in the mouth and cancelled in the hands.

When she spoke again, her voice smelt like rain before it happens. "Don't ever lie to me," she said. "Not even to make it easier."

"I'm not—" he started, and she watched his face choose a crossroads she hadn't offered him. His mouth closed. He swallowed. He looked, for a breath, like a boy who wished he were good and a boy who wished he were free.

"Tell me you won't see her again," she said.

He didn't answer.

The silence was a chapter break written in sky.

They stood inside an echo. The field's edges darkened to bruised violet, the first stars arriving like an audience unwilling to applaud. From the far side of the track, the thud of a stray basketball rose and fell, someone practising alone the way some people prayed.

"You didn't kiss her," Melody said, almost to herself. "I saw that. You didn't touch."

"That's true."

"It looked like you had your hands on each other anyway."

"Mel."

"I'm tired of being generous for both of us," she said. It came out like a confession to a sin she didn't believe was wrong.

"Then don't be."

"That's not the relief you think it is."

He put his hands in his pockets. The gesture made him look young again; it also made her want to empty those pockets onto the grass and inventory every last proof of the day. When he spoke next, his voice was careful. "I'm not choosing Charlotte. You know that, right?"

"Do I?"

"Yes."

"Then choose me," she said. "Here. Now. Say it like a vow. Not that I'm the best so far. Not that I make you better. Say you're mine."

Something flickered across his face—fear, maybe; or its dignified cousin, self-preservation. He didn't look away. He also didn't move closer. "I can say I love you," he said. "It's true. I do. But the other thing—the ownership thing—you know that's not what I can promise."

The night moved a fraction. In the bleachers beyond the field, a trio of girls shouted and then, catching themselves in their own echo, fell into delighted giggles that cut the air like glass and then dissolved. A moth stuttered around the bulb over the back door of the school, battering itself against the idea of light.

"You're using the good words to cover the bad choices," she said.

"You're squeezing the good words until they can't breathe."

"And she—what is she doing? Practising being kind in ways that look like permission?"

He scrubbed his palm over his face, as if he could wake himself into a version of this where everyone behaved with noble simplicity. "You're making a monster out of someone who isn't one."

Melody thought of Charlotte's soft cross, her careful hands, the symmetrical life that made other people's chaos feel like a personal failing. She thought of the way goodness is a currency and people spend it to buy what they want while calling it grace.

"My mother introduced her to you," she said. "You both came to my house and drank from my glasses and then you sat with her in public like you were being transparent while you built something you didn't want to name."

He flinched. "We had a coffee. You're inventing a conspiracy."

"I've seen the way you lean," she said softly. "It's a language."

"Then translate this: I'm done fighting about imaginary crimes." His voice stayed low. Exhaustion pulled at the edges. "If every time I talk to another person, I'm on trial—"

"You weren't talking to another person," she said. "You were talking to the woman who watched me learn to be good and decided to practise your future against the example of it."

He was quiet for a long time, and in the quiet she heard the creak in the third stair at home, the small ways a house tells you it remembers you even when people forget to. When he spoke, it was to the ground. "I miss who we were at the beginning. I miss driving nowhere and feeling like that was a destination."

"You could still choose that."

"I could," he said. And then: "But not if choosing it means vanishing into you."

Something inside her tilted toward a ledge she hadn't known was there. This was the part where she said, I hear you, I will take a breath, let light into the jar. This was the part where she opened her fists. Instead she thought about the cold of the window glass against her forehead the night she'd asked love to make her holy. She thought of the answer that hadn't been a sound so much as a permission.

She stepped forward until they were close enough to share breath. "Do you love me?"

"Yes," he said. It came easy; it always had.

"Then let that be bigger than your fear."

"My fear," he said, and something in him lifted its head. "You scare me because I don't recognise myself when I'm with you. You don't leave room for me to be anyone but the person you're writing down in your notebooks. It's like you're building a shrine to me and then punishing me for not worshipping at it the way you do."

She almost said, I *am* worshipping. But the past tense snagged her. She pulled back a little, tried to fit his words against the structure she'd built. "I want to keep us safe," she said, shocked by how small the truth sounded when spoken aloud.

"From what?"

"From other people," she whispered.

"From me being a person," he replied.

Silence arrived and sat between them with its hands folded.

He reached for her waist. The gesture was familiar, tender, a cue in a dance they had perfected. She should have melted into it, forgiven the world, believed the colder truths were tricks of light. But the image of the café returned—condensation sliding down, that fern-shadow threading pattern onto Charlotte's wrist—and instead of sweetness, a heat rose in her chest so clean she could taste its metal.

"Don't," she said, stepping back.

"Okay," he said, wary.

"Just tell me," she asked, softer now, almost pleading, "that you won't see her again."

He didn't move. He didn't answer.

The stars were louder than breath. A car on the far road exhaled its way into a corner and out again. Somewhere, a dog—honest and unbothered by metaphor—barked once, twice, announcing itself to the night.

"Nick," she said, his name a thread she had wound too many times around the same finger. "Please."

He lifted his shoulders—a shrug that performed mercy and delivered refusal. "I won't promise that."

It was such a small sentence. It had the weight of a falling leaf. And yet when it landed, it cracked something that had been waiting all along to be decided about.

She didn't remember deciding. She remembered the white flare, the way the field filmed over as if she were underwater for a breath and the surface had become story. She remembered the sound her hand made meeting his cheek—not a movie slap, not the stingy pop of theatre, but a soft, wet sound, like a fish moved too quickly from one body of water to another.

After, the quiet was so complete the world felt briefly uninhabited.

He didn't step back. He didn't lift a hand to his face. He blinked, slow, the way you blink when light betrays you.

Her palm burned. In its heat, shame and relief crowded, siblings jostling for the same chair.

"Mel," he said at last, voice low and clean of ornament. "That's not who you are."

She wanted to say, *You don't get to decide that.* She wanted to say, *You made me into the shape of what you required, and now you blame me for fitting.* She wanted to say anything but what came out: "I'm sorry."

She was and she wasn't. The apology floated between them like a moth and pointed itself toward a bulb that had already burned out.

He nodded once, as if to a fact he had suspected but hoped to avoid. His cheek had pinked, the mark rising like a small country accepting its borders. "I think I have to go," he said.

She did not reach for him. She had learned, in some old part of herself, that reaching announces need and need invites cruelty. She stood still and tried to hold the world in place by the power of refusal. It didn't work. It never had. He turned and the field agreed with him, making a path of his leaving that the grass would stay pressed about for minutes after as if remembering.

She listened to his footsteps until they became memory. She waited for the sound of a car door, an engine. She waited for the night to close the door behind him. When it did, it did not latch.

The field returned to itself—crickets resuming their unembarrassed chorus, a small wind rubbing cool hands over bruised heat. In the school's high windows, her reflection was a faint ghost, the kind that lingers even after you've convinced yourself you've stopped believing in such things.

She looked down at her hand. The linework of her life—palm, fate, heart— hadn't altered. She pressed the stinging skin to her lips the way you do when you've touched a pan you knew was hot and did it anyway.

The urge to run—to his house, to hers, to anywhere there was a door she could shut and lean against—rose and passed. Instead she walked to the edge of the field where the metal bleachers sat like a ship run aground. She sat on the bottom rung and felt the cool of it enter her bones.

Above the track, moths kept hurling themselves at the dumb, continuous promise of the light. Each impact made a small, soundless punctuation she could feel in her teeth.

She tried, briefly, to imagine tomorrow as if it were a thing that could be negotiated with. She tried to imagine being softer, less large, the kind of girl who could say go if you need to and mean it, the kind of girl who could read the coffee as nothing and the distance as growing pains. She tried and the trying moved through her like a prayer spoken in a language she didn't understand.

When she finally stood, the grass left a pattern on the backs of her calves. The night had grown fragrant—honeysuckle somewhere, insistent and indecent. She breathed it in like medicine and tasted sugar and rot at once.

Walking home, she avoided the streets with porch lights and wide windows. She took the long cuts—beside the chain-link fence where wild morning glory pretended to be tame, along the alley where the bins were lined up like soldiers who'd forgotten which war they were in. At the last corner before her house, she stopped and looked up because the sky had decided to be generous with its stars. They looked close enough to touch and too far to save.

In the kitchen, the oven light blinked—someone had set a timer hours ago and not turned it off. On the table, Valerie had left a plate wrapped in beeswax cloth—chicken, a baked potato with a cross cut in its back like a blessing, a wedge of lemon that had made a pale sun on the paper. The care in it was so naked she almost had to look away.

Upstairs, she washed her face too hard and watched her skin bloom with reprimand in the mirror. The girl in the glass was beautiful in the precise, thoughtless way good lighting makes anything look like grace. She didn't trust her.

She opened the window and knelt. It was not prayer. It was inventory. Night. Heat. A far siren arguing with distance. The shape of what she had done. The shape of what had been done to her. The shape of what was coming that she could feel approaching like weather.

Across the street, a cat stepped along the top of a fence with the uncowed confidence of a creature who had never doubted its right to be anywhere. She envied the cat its small, exactified purpose.

Behind her, the door clicked softly. "Mel?" Valerie's voice, careful as a plate with a hairline crack. "You're home."

"I'm fine," Melody said without turning.

A pause, a mother listening past the words. "I left you dinner."

"Thank you."

Another small quiet. "I love you."

"I know."

She heard the hallway breathe as Valerie left, the carpet accepting the weight it was made to accept. Melody kept kneeling, the night pressing its steady palm against her fever. In the corner of the room, his jacket hung on the chair like a body that had forgotten it wasn't one.

She didn't cry. The tears stayed where they were made: at the bottom of the lake she had built in herself to hold him. The surface was very calm.

When she finally rose, she went to her journal and wrote with a hand that didn't belong to any child she had ever been: *He says I scare him when he loses sight of himself. What I wanted to say: I'm only a mirror. What I didn't write: if a mirror shows you a monster, don't blame the glass.*

She closed the book gently, as if tucking a baby in. As she turned off the lamp, the room flattened back into shadow. The window stayed open, the night moving through it, slow and sure, the way water learns a house and then a house learns water.

Outside, somewhere just beyond town, a train laid its long note across the dark. It sounded like a line drawn with a hard pencil, like a decision that had already been made and was in the act of revealing itself. Melody stood very still and let the sound pass through her, emptying out everything it could reach.

When it was gone, she whispered into the room—not to God, not to love, not to any solvable thing: "Mine."

The word did not echo. It didn't need to. It sat where she placed it—the first stone in a path the night could see even if she could not.

The Discovery

For three days the town wore a heat it hadn't earned. It pressed its palm over Reading and made everything shine with a damp, needless intensity—mailboxes sweating, porch swings too hot to touch, dogs lying in doorways with their tongues lolling like surrender flags. It was the kind of weather that made tempers short and hours long. It made Melody's skin feel wrong, too present on her body, like a dress she'd borrowed from someone who wanted it back.

She went to school. She sat in classes that felt like dioramas—people arranged in small, plausible scenes. She sang in choir without hearing herself and nodded at Brooke's questions as if nodding were a language. She moved through days like a person walking along a pier after dark: straight, careful, convinced of water on either side. When her teachers asked if everything was all right, she said of course and filled the space with a smile that behaved like furniture—solid, utilitarian, meant to be looked at and set aside.

Inside, there was only one sound: her heart. It had become a drum that belonged to no band. It beat in her wrists when she lifted her pencil, in her throat when she swallowed, in her teeth when she tried to sleep. Sometimes she would think of Nick's name and the rhythm would change, stutter, then race, as if memory were a conductor she'd offended. She had watched him leave. The field had forgiven them and the moths had kept their appointment with the light. The ordinary had stayed ordinary, which felt like an insult.

On the fourth evening, the heat broke without rain. The clouds gathered and argued, then wandered off, leaving the sky smelling metallic, like a promise not kept. Melody stood at her window and tried to bargain with the air. She told herself she would not text him. She told herself she would let love be bigger than her fear, and then wondered if this—this hunger, this ache, this refusal to let the world move without her consent—was what people meant when they said fear.

Downstairs, her mother moved through the kitchen, making summer food: cucumbers in salt water, tomatoes in a glass bowl like small hearts without bodies, a roast chicken gone cool enough to tear. Melody listened to the small busy sounds—drawers opened and closed, a knife knocking politely against a board—and she wanted them the way she wanted oxygen: automatic, unearned, always there.

"Dinner," Valerie called up the stairs, voice hoarse from a day of not saying the things she wanted to.

"I'm not hungry," Melody answered, already beginning to lie in the ways that would prove she was someone new.

"You haven't eaten since lunch."

"I'm fine."

She wasn't, but fine had always been a door she knew the code to. She opened it, stepped through, closed it quietly behind her, and turned the lock.

*　*　*　*　*

Her phone lay face down on the desk. She had started doing that lately—turning things so their faces were hidden. The jacket, the framed photo from the fair, the Polaroids with edges worn pale from her thumbs. If a thing could look at you, it could accuse you. She didn't want to be accused by anything that didn't understand.

She waited for the first vibration like a woman waiting for thunder. It didn't come. She flipped the phone over anyway, the action as involuntary as a flinch. Nothing—then, as if humiliated by its own tardiness, a message arrived.

Hey. Can we talk?

She stared at the three words until they blurred. Can we talk, as if talk were a place they could go without consequence. As if talk were not a blade too often mistaken for a key.

Where? she typed, and deleted, and typed again, and deleted. The drum in her chest shifted tempo. She put the phone face down. She picked it up. She put it down again. She stood. She sat. She laughed once, out loud, because the room had become a waiting room and she had not made an appointment.

A second message arrived, as though he had seen her not-answering and decided to be the one who knew how to move forward.

I can swing by later. Or tomorrow.

Later. Tomorrow. Words that pretended to be patient but were really only dressed in delay. She closed her eyes and saw the café instead of her desk —the condensation sliding, the fern-shadow on Charlotte's wrist, the way the world had tilted and then insisted it remained level. She wrote back: *not tonight. busy*. Then added, before she could behave: *don't see her*.

A minute passed. Two. A third arrived, slow as a late train. *You don't get to tell me who to see, Melody.*

Her thumb hovered over the keyboard. She typed *I do* and deleted it. She typed *I don't want to tell you* and changed it to then *don't make me*. She deleted that too and set the phone down, face-up now, because it felt worse to pretend she wasn't watching.

He didn't say anything else.

That night she slept for twenty minutes at a time, snatched naps that tasted like stale mints and old dreams. She woke to the sound of a motorcycle somewhere far away, to the faint swish of a car turning a corner politely, to Max getting up to pee and the toilet's obedient sigh. She woke on the hour and at the half-hour, her brain choosing numbers as if they mattered—1:30, 2:00, 2:30, a procession of halves and wholes like the world mocking calculus.

At 3:12 a.m., in the country where decisions are born, she sat up. The room looked like it belonged to someone else. A girl whose life had been printed in clean lines and now smudged by a wet thumb. She swung her legs over the side of the bed and the laminate floor gave up a small coolness that felt like advice.

She went to her desk and opened the drawer where she kept a small bundle of things she wasn't supposed to have—a pin to pop SIM trays, a thumb drive she'd once told herself she might use for a school project, a spare charging cable, a folded paper with a list of things Nick had said that she'd written down not because she liked to catalogue but because cataloguing made them real. On the bottom of the list, a date. His birthday. She had believed, at the time, that remembering it was the same as loving well.

She held the paper for a moment, the way you hold a photograph of someone who has learned how to smile without you. Then she folded it again, sharp, lined the edges precisely, and put it back.

She did not own his phone. She knew that. She told herself so in the firm voice schools used for rules about hall passes. She also knew he kept his passcode simple, a habit born of carelessness and small-town optimism. Birthdays. Band names. Palindromes he liked the sound of. Once he had boasted that the only thing he needed to remember was his birthday— you'd be shocked how many things that unlocks—and the memory of his laugh then made her want to strike a match.

She didn't have his phone. She had her phone. But the two of them had sat so often in the blue-lit intimacy of his car, devices on their thighs, thumbs moving in companionable silence, that she could see his lock screen as if it were a painting hung in her own hallway. If she closed her eyes, she could watch his numbers appear under his thumb—0, 8, 3, 3, the year, the day, the month; she could see the way he'd swipe and grin and say *privacy is for people with something to hide* and she had thought, then, that it was charm. Now it felt like a dare.

She told herself she would not do it. She told herself she would sleep. She told herself she would answer him in the morning with a message so clean and reasonable that any judge, anywhere, would sing her praises and stamp her paper with the seal of sanity.

Instead, at 3:27, she went downstairs for water and stood at the sink gulping from a glass like someone newly rescued. The house was the particular quiet of summer night—the fridge ticking its private language, the wind making a curtain sigh, the clock over the stove casting its faint, dictatorial green. On the counter, Valerie had left her phone charging, the cord looping in a neat, maternal question mark.

For a second, a ridiculous thought: that a mother's phone might be a measure of the world. That opening it would show you how to be. She touched it the way you touch a sleeping person you love—careful, almost superstitious. The screen woke, revealed the wallpaper: Max at six with ice cream on his mouth, Valerie's hand on his shoulder just out of frame. Melody felt an ache so sudden she made a sound without meaning to, a small broken word that wasn't a word at all.

She set it down. She lifted her own phone. She went back upstairs.

On her desk, the notebook lay open from the night before. You can break a heart with nothing but silence, she had written in a heat that now embarrassed her. She closed the book, put the phone on top, and watched the thin, stubborn light in the seam where the cover didn't quite meet the pages. She felt like that—almost closed. Not closed.

At 3:41, she texted Nick: *Can I borrow your charger?* Mine is acting up. It was the oldest trick in the world and the newest. He didn't reply. She watched the message sit there, thin as a fishing line without a bobber. Then she typed again: *Door?* and got *I'm asleep* back, which made her laugh in a single rude burst, because people love to narrate their own inattention as if you should thank them for it.

Please, she wrote. *5 minutes.*

A long minute this time. Then: *Back door's open. My mom's sleeping. Don't wake the dog.*

She stared at the words. They made a shape in her mind she recognised: a path. She put on shorts and his jacket because the jacket had become a habit her body understood better than honesty. She slipped her feet into shoes and left the house the way ghosts do: seeing everything, moving nothing.

Reading at 4 a.m. is a different country. The traffic lights become devotional—red, yellow, green rotating above empty intersections like saints undecided. The birds start practising their morning before the morning agrees to arrive. The houses look embarrassed by their daytime lives—porches groaning, siding dull, garden gnomes like drunk uncles sleeping it off. Melody walked through it all with her hands in her pockets and her mouth in a line, another pilgrim among many, doing a thing the daylight would insist she deny.

Nick's back gate stuck, the way it always had, with a small metal squeal that sounded like a scold. She lifted it a fraction and slid through, the gesture as familiar as opening her own locker. The kitchen window gave back a faint, forgiving light; the clock over their stove was the same dictatorial green. The back door—propped with a brick, half ajar, as promised—breathed a little when she touched it.

Inside, the house smelt like laundry and dog and a lemon cleaner that acted like a good deed. The dog—a fat beagle named Henry who had never decided whether to trust her—lay on his side and lifted an eyelid, then let it fall again, exhausted by his own permissiveness. Melody paused at the bottom of the stairs and listened. Silence, rich as velvet. She climbed, counting without wanting to: one, two, three—creak—four, five, six—the small landing—seven, eight, nine, and then the short hall to his room.

His door was half closed. His room looked the way boys' rooms look when they trust gravity to clean up after them—clothes in an unapologetic pile, guitar leaning like a soldier on leave, notebooks in a stack as tall as a decision. He slept on his side, mouth open, arm flung out, vulnerable in the unhandsome way that made her love him more. His phone lay on the table beside the bed, tethered to the wall like a boat.

She stood there, so close the breath moving in and out of him fluttered the cuff of her shorts, and felt a tenderness so acute it must have had a twin. She wanted to touch his face, wake him into a version of the truth where everything could be said and forgiven in the same sentence. She wanted, too, to be unforgiving, to be the person who did the thing and lived with it, because living with it felt easier than living with the guessing.

The phone showed the time like a dare. 4:19. She unplugged it with a politeness that enraged her. It woke in her hand. She held her own phone on top of it, bright over black, as if one could bless the other.

There is a way your thumb learns another person's numbers. Muscle memory is a love language. She typed. She got red denial, the soft thud of no. She tried again, another permutation of the year and day, another old symmetry he liked because it made the world look planned. No. She tried the name of his first band; no. She tried the number on the jersey he never wore; no.

Her heart changed rhythm. The drum became a flock of birds, lifting all at once at an unseen signal. She looked at him sleeping—at the lashes she'd once envied, at the mouth that had ruined her for ever wanting to be ruined by anyone else—and she felt the exact shape of the line she was crossing. Then she stepped over it.

She entered his birthday backwards. The screen opened the way a mouth opens to tell you it's over.

For a second, she only stood there, the way a person stands at the edge of a lake before winter, unbelieving of how water can be a floor. Then she scrolled.

In the dim, the icons were hieroglyphics. She touched Photos because that's where people keep the evidence of their own narratives. Albums— Recents, Favourites, Camera Roll, a folder labelled Tour that was aspirational to the point of comedy. She opened Recents and the world tipped, the bed seeming to slide a degree toward the wall, the lamp leaning like it had entered a new field of devotion, everything joining her in the tilt.

Charlotte's room. Something she knew with certainty, even thought she'd never seen it. At first, too close—a slice of white sheet, a curve of pale wrist, a book open and face down as if interrupted by something more interesting than reading. Another: the window that faced an old maple outside her dorm, leaves making noise with the light, and on the sill a small ceramic dish with rings in it, one of them a thin gold band that wasn't a promise but thought it was. Another: the bed made, the coverlet a Scandinavian neutral that made her think of snow that never took footprints.

Then not the room: Charlotte herself, shoulders bare, hair down, the kind of light that pretends it isn't trying. Not naked, not obscene; the modesty of a person who knows what you'll do with your imagination and offers you a little help. She wasn't looking at the camera. She was looking at something beyond it—someone, just to the left, just out of frame. There was affection in her mouth, not a smile, something more serious. The date stamp in the corner felt like a verdict—it belonged to the week between coffee and field, a day that had worn ordinary clothes while planning a party behind her back.

Melody tried to breathe and the air was a different element now, too thin or too heavy—wrong, whatever it was. She scrolled again, a compulsion and a cruelty. Another photo: Nick's hand (she knew it as well as she knew her own) holding a book open on Charlotte's bed, the pages dappled by the window-fern. His knuckles ink-marked. His denim knee in the corner of the frame, careless as intimacy sometimes is. Another: a bowl of sliced pears, a cup of tea on a saucer, a mess of notes in two handwritings—his scrawl, her tidy sermon—proof that you can build a life in small violations.

Not a single kiss. Not a single obscene thing the world could call obscene. Nothing you could take to court except the way proximity becomes permission when people trust you to read the room as chaste. It would be possible to stand in this spot, phone in hand, and say, No crime. It would be possible to take a breath and give back the night without breaking anything else. It would be possible, if you were someone else.

Below the photos, a screen capture of a text thread. She told herself not to touch it and then touched it. A message from him: *you look like a painting no one should be allowed to own.* Her reply: *You could own me. You could do whatever you want with me.* A photo of a book spine. Another of the inside of a wrist with a smear of ink and then another screen capture of a text thread: *Your fault, poet.* A voice note she would not play, because she was not that kind of cruel—not yet—and because some sounds, once heard, take up residence in the walls.

She closed Photos. She opened the Notes app, because he sometimes treated it like a pocket. Lyrics, fragments, a list titled things to be good at —listening, not lying, leaving. She stared at the last word until the meaning lifted off it like steam and left nothing but shape. She closed the app. She should have put the phone down then, plugged it back in, left the house, gone home. She should have put her face on her pillow and taken the night in her teeth and torn it. She did not.

She went to Messages. She scrolled past her own thread, bright and greedy; past Ben and his no punctuation; past his mother's reminders to take the chicken out of the freezer; and there it was: C.

C for Charlotte. Not even a full name. The respect of an initial. The efficiency of knowing.

She touched the thread and the conversation opened like a curtain. Small things that were not small—a photo of the river from the hill where she had kissed him first, taken from a different angle, as if that mattered. A link to a song with a title that made its own case for doom. Her words reading like restraint, his reading like trying. *You're easy to talk to*, he'd written. *Don't ruin that. I won't*, she'd replied. *I don't break good things*, Charlotte wrote, saintly as always, and Melody felt contempt roll through her like a wave in slow motion, foam with its own elegance.

She closed the thread, thumb trembling not from guilt but from the body's rebellion against what the mind had decided it could bear. She stared at the time—4:33—and thought, wildly, of her mother's cake timer. She stood there with his phone in her hand and realised her body had been learning this moment for months.

There are some discoveries that make the world larger. This was the other kind. The room shrank. The bed, the desk, the window—their dimensions rushed inward, as if space itself were jealous. She put the phone down too carefully and the cord slipped from the table's edge with a soft defenceless sound. She caught it. She plugged it in. She stood over him a moment more, because she was human and therefore needed to hurt herself as close to the source as possible.

Nick shifted in his sleep and made a small, honest noise—the kind people only make when their bodies are sure they are safe. It cracked something —and the crack was not loud; it was a hairline fracture in the glaze of a beautiful bowl that meant you could keep drinking from it if you pretended not to mind the way liquid found a way out.

She left the room. The third stair creaked like an accomplice. At the bottom, the dog opened his eyes and considered an opinion, then returned to his dream. The back door's hinge confessed to the night and the gate squealed again, as if to tell someone—anyone—that a girl had taught herself to be a weather system.

Outside, the air had gone clear. The sky was on the cusp of admitting morning—pale at the edges, uncertain in the middle. A train laid a long sound across the dark, and it felt like a pencil drawing a line so straight even the landscape agreed to it. She walked home through alleys that smelt like warm metal and wildflowers pretending to be weeds, and by the time she reached her block she had talked herself through every position: that it was innocent, that it was cruel, that it was nothing, that it was everything. By the time she climbed her own stairs, she had come to the conclusion that felt most like oxygen: that she had been right to love as large as she did, and that the world punished largeness by mistaking it for violence.

Her room was the same room she had left. The heat had gathered again while she was gone, a small tyranny. She turned on the lamp and the light made the walls into theatre flats—prettier, shallower, easy to move. She went to the desk, opened the notebook, smoothed the paper with a palm that finally shook.

At first nothing came. The drum had stopped. The birds had landed. The conductor had thrown his arms up and gone home. Melody stared at the blank and saw not Charlotte's bare shoulders, not Nick's knee in the corner of a frame, not the way a fern can etch its autograph onto skin. She saw herself kneeling at the window, the night's breath on her face, the vow she'd made to love itself because God was too small to manage this.

Her hand began to move.

She did not write about birthdays or passwords or photos that pretended to be art. She did not write about the dog or the stair. She did not write the words that might be read aloud in a room of people who could be persuaded not to worry. She wrote the truth she could live inside. Her handwriting was slow and neat, a courtesy she refused to abandon.

She wrote: *She took what was mine. She thought she could love my love better than me. Don't blame me for what comes next.*

Part II

The Crime

The Drive

The storm arrived the way gossip does in a small town—first as a rumour in the leaves, then as a certainty that made the air taste metallic. By late afternoon, Reading had closed one eye against the sky and braced. The humidity went from impolite to indecent. Flags on porches hung like wet tongues. Somewhere beyond the hill, thunder rehearsed its lines.

Melody waited until the first drop hit the kitchen window with the precision of a thrown pebble. She stood in the doorway long enough to hear the house register the change—Valerie's voice quieting mid-sentence, the dog in the next yard making a single interrogative bark, the refrigerator taking a breath before shouldering on.

She took her father's keys from the ceramic dish by the door, the one shaped like a leaf. The keys were warm with the house's heat. They jangled in her palm like a handful of small, bright decisions.

"Where are you going?" Valerie called from the stovetop, though her tone said: tell me something I can bless.

"Just for a walk," Melody said, palming her father's car keys, knowing she was a long way off from her license and being allowed to drive. "To think."

"In the rain?" Valerie had asked, her head tilting sideways. A pause, then the soft admission that comes from knowing she didn't fully understand her daughter, but not knowing how to untangle the problem of adolescents: "Come home."

"I will," Melody had said with a sweet smile, her hands clutching car keys behind her back.

She didn't add when. She didn't add who she would be when she did.

Outside, the storm darkened the street one degree at a time, as if someone were lowering a dimmer the town didn't know it had. The first rain came tentative, an audition. Then the sky committed. Water ran off the eaves in sheets; the asphalt shone black as a pupil. Trees bowed as if the wind had remembered something about them and decided to test it.

She slid into her father's car—his reliable old sedan that smelt faintly of coffee, lumber, and the peppermints he kept in the console. She adjusted the seat back. Mirror, belt, hands at ten and two. The keys fit like a confession. The engine turned and the dashboard lit up with its mild little mercies: fuel enough, oil fine, doors closed, you are held. The wipers began their morse-code insistence—yes not-yet yes not-yet yes.

She pulled away from the curb and felt the world loosen from her in a way that wasn't freedom so much as release. The storm wrapped the car in its busy privacy. Sound simplified to three elements: the percussion of rain, the deep-belly thuds of thunder, the low animal hum of the engine. Everything else—the neighbour's wind chimes, the shouts from the basketball hoop at the end of the block, the dog naming each passer-by— was cancelled by weather.

Water braided itself down the windshield, the glass becoming a living thing. Each sweep of the wipers granted her a second of clarity, then took it back. Her face flickered in the rear-view, a ghost trying on a girl.

"If love is faith," she whispered to the empty car, "I'm devout."

The words steadied her more than any seat belt could. They made shape inside her chest. Devotion had rules. Devotion gave people something to do with their hands. The radio tried to offer a song and she turned it off, not wanting anyone else's narrative contaminating hers. The storm would sing. She would listen.

She took Ninth past the school, where the track glistened like a coin and the bleachers wore a dark sheen. She made the turn by the thrift store with the window of cowboy boots and saints, spared a glance for the pair the colour of honey she'd once wanted and now could not imagine ever wearing. At each red light, the rain thickened the air between her and the world into a curtain she could step behind and choose a different face to show. She chose the one with the steady mouth.

She passed Crux Café. Through the rain-lacquered windows she could see shapes—shoulders, a hand lifting a cup, a barista dragging a rag across the counter like penance. The plant in the window drooped with overwatering, a jungle in miniature. She did not slow down. She watched it all smear and then reassemble in the side mirror in a little theatre of regret.

The storm nosed at the car, testing, pushing. She gripped the wheel and the wheel gripped back. Water pooled at the edges of the road where the drains were lazy. A cyclist balanced between bravado and foolishness, hood up, legs pumping, the thin tires knifing lines into the wet that were gone, almost before he'd made them. Lightning stitched white through the clouds and made the world's bones visible for an instant. She felt the flash in her teeth.

"If love is faith, I'm devout," she repeated. The sentence took on a rhythm. On the third iteration, she laughed—a small, startled sound that sounded too loud in the wet cave of the car. On the fourth, the laugh cracked and she cried. Tears came clean at first, then hot, then salt that stung the chapped edges of her mouth. She did not try to stop. The wipers kept time for her grief.

She took the bridge over the river slow; the guardrail was a slick promise. The Schuylkill below writhed—brown, muscled, annoyed at being asked to carry so much sky all at once. In the brief clarity between swipes, she could see the surface convulsing—rain making a million impacts, each a small insistence, together a doctrine.

She drove with the instincts of a person who knows a town by its hazards— the manhole that always lifted in a flood, the dip by the red brick church where cars became brief boats, the corner that collected the confetti of shredded leaves and made them into a slippery sermon. She navigated each and felt herself sharpen by it, the way a blade sharpens because someone has decided to draw it along a stone.

The dorms at Alvernia rose out of the rain like ships—not grand ones, not liners, but sturdy ferries that had crossed the same distance so often even their rust had learned to be polite. Brick darkened by weather. Windows like orderly eyes. The small plaque by the hedges announcing the building's name with collegiate self-importance. She knew the back lot where the lighting was lax and the sightlines forgiving. She knew the way the dumpsters made a wall and the maple beyond the corner offered cover with its scandalous leaves.

She turned off Lancaster and slid into the campus. The storm seemed to lower itself, not over the buildings but around her, a cloak. Students moved in it in pairs, hunched, laughing, heads ducked, bodies slaloming between drops that did not care to be dodged. Backpacks clung to shoulders like small, worried children. Someone in a bright yellow slicker stood on the stoop letting the rain hit their face, the way some people enter the ocean—mouth open, arms out, convinced they can be made new by contact.

Melody circled once to be sure. The back lot was mostly empty—one white sedan like a tooth, a maintenance van, a blue hatchback beaded with a thousand miniature storms. She parked with deliberate imprecision, not in a space. The car's flank tucked behind the shoulder of a dumpster. The engine's hum died when she told it to. Thunder took up the slack.

She sat with both hands still on the wheel, fingers printed white. Her heart had rearranged itself from drum to bell: not beating but tolling. She listened to it. She let it ring in her throat, her wrists, the soft place at the base of her skull.

As Melody sat there, the dorm's back door exhaled one of its small, habitual sighs—the pneumatic hinge releasing the weight it had agreed to bear. A girl in a hoodie slipped out, sprinted the ten metres to the white car, slid in, and became a silhouette doing something—dabbing at her face with a sleeve? changing a song? texting someone who thought the rain would forgive what they planned?—before reversing too fast and splashing a hedge with a fan of water.

Melody watched the door close again and become a rectangle: lit, indifferent, the wet footprints on the linoleum just inside already thinking about evaporating. This was where Charlotte went in and out. This was where goodness had learned the choreography of secrecy. This was the hinge of the story.

She lifted a hand from the wheel and saw the tremor. It travelled the length of her forearm, found her elbow, kept going. She did not will it away. She watched it, curious, like a scientist looking through a lens at a specimen that might reveal something about the world if she stared long enough.

Her reflection quivered in the driver's window—double-exposed by raindrop and streetlight, a choir of selves singing over each other. In one she looked furious. In another, sanctified. In a third, only a girl in a car in a storm.

"Charlotte," she said, testing the name in the small public square of the car. The rain applauded. "Charlotte."

It was not a curse. It was a diagnosis. It was the name of the place where the map had been redrawn without asking her if she wanted to live there.

She closed her eyes and saw the photos as if she had taken them: pear slices with a knife left pointed toward the edge of the plate; the tidy rings in a dish, two combined and one apart; the window's fern printing its pattern onto the wrist that rested too close to where his words kept their heat. She opened her eyes and the world had the decency to be the same as the one she'd closed them on.

She wiped her face with the heel of her hand, not to erase tears but to acknowledge them. Rain turned her hand cold in a second. Her breath fogged the glass near the seam of the window. She wrote, without meaning to, a line with her fingertip—one short, one long, a private notation that meant nothing and everything: *I am here.*

Thunder laid its body over the buildings again, long and low, so close she could hear the chuff at its end, like a great beast amused by its own power. Lightning followed so fast it didn't bother being a surprise. The brick went white, then red again. The windows blinked. For a heartbeat, the maple held a thousand silver threads and then dropped them all.

Her phone lay face-up in the cup holder, gathering a wet confetti of drops that sneaked through the door's rubber will and found a way. No new messages. No small blue bubbles working at an apology. She put the phone face down. She didn't need witnesses for the next minutes. She didn't need pardon. She needed to move.

She unbuckled. The sound of the belt withdrawing was a zipper unseaming something. She rested her hands in her lap. They were not steady. The tremor had become an articulate stutter—each finger with its own grammar of want.

"If love is faith," she said one more time, because a creed works by repetition, "I'm devout."

The storm obligingly wrote a new line of rain down the glass to underline it.

She reached for the door handle and paused. It wasn't hesitation. It was ceremony. She looked at the dorm. She pictured the corridor with its bulletin board announcing a bake sale that had already happened, the smell of hot dust when the radiator came on in January, the communal sigh of ten doors shutting the same hour on the same weeknight. She pictured Charlotte's room as if she'd been there: the bed made with that Nordic neatness that pretends it isn't pride, the window she'd seen from his photos, the dish of rings, the book face down and trusting, the small cross on the nightstand that made goodness into a talisman instead of a practice. She pictured the exact hinge of the moment to come—the lift of an eyebrow, the intake of breath, the sound a voice makes when it believes itself unassailable and learns otherwise.

Rain hammered the roof of the car and made a noise like a thousand whispers agreeing. The air smelt like pennies and wet stone and something green that could not be contained. Her hands shook harder.

She closed her fingers into fists and felt the ache of muscle and bone, the life in them. She held them in front of her face, the way a boxer looks at what he's brought to the ring. They weren't weapons. They were the ends of her vows, the punctuation for everything she had said to the dark when the dark seemed to be listening.

She opened the door. The storm leaned in, intimate. Water touched her face like an old friend. The world outside was all percussion and flash—no melody, only rhythm. She stepped out into it, small and exact, and the rain pinned her hair to her temples and soaked Nick's jacket through in a second so that it clung to her like his presence. She shut the door quietly—devotion isn't loud—and stood there with the car at her back and the dorm in front of her, and her fists trembling in the generous, relentless rain.

The Confrontation

The rain had changed from downpour to percussion, the sort that plays on every surface at once—roof, gutter, leaf, skin—until the whole city seems to pulse to the same exhausted beat. Melody crossed the lot beneath it, water coursing down her arms, her shoes giving small aquatic sighs with each step.

The dorm's back door yielded easily, as though some small god of coincidence had decided to grant her passage. The corridor beyond smelt of soap and metal and that faint, electric scent of overworked wiring. Fluorescent light buzzed overhead, a constant, insectile harmony. She could hear the hum of refrigerators in the communal kitchen, the whisper of televisions behind closed doors. Each sound felt borrowed, as though the world were lending her a few more ordinary seconds before something irreparable.

Charlotte's door was the third on the right—name tag curling, polite handwriting spelling *C. Nilsson.* The letters shimmered under the hall light, trembling a little with the draft from the stairwell. Melody lifted her hand and knocked. Once. Twice.

The door opened on the third.

Charlotte stood there wrapped in a pale robe, the fabric damp at the shoulders where steam from the shower had touched it. Her hair, that impossible blond that always looked borrowed from a halo, hung darkened and heavy down her back. Surprise crossed her face first—then concern, not fear.

"Melody?" The name landed gently, like a towel offered. "You're soaked.

Come in before—"

Melody didn't move for what felt like hours. The hallway light threw both their reflections onto the polished floor, two versions of the same girl— one calm, one trembling slightly around the edges. "I thought you were going home for the summer?" Melody finally managed.

Charlotte's eyes darted away and then back to Melody's. "Come in," she repeated.

Melody entered the dorm, closing the door behind herself.

"Do you love him?" The words arrived raw, stripped of ceremony.

Charlotte blinked, confusion flaring, then fading into something like pity. "Nick?"

The silence that followed answered for her. It lasted exactly as long as the roll of thunder outside.

"I didn't mean—" Charlotte began, and the sentence came out soft, apologetic. "I never wanted to hurt you. I just thought—he said you were —" She stopped herself, as if mercy were still possible. "I'm sorry. Truly. You're very young. I feel for you."

That tone—that gentle, condescending sympathy—was worse than confession. It was forgiveness offered before guilt had even drawn breath.

Melody felt the air in the corridor change pressure. The lights flickered, or maybe that was her vision. Somewhere down the hall a door opened and closed, laughter spilled, and was swallowed again. The rain grew louder until it became indistinguishable from breathing.

Charlotte reached out as if to steady her. "Let's talk," she said. "Please. You're shivering."

The gesture—open palm, immaculate nails—might have been an act of kindness in another story. In this one, it was a trigger.

The next moments folded in on themselves like wet paper. A flash of white light from the window, a sound that could have been thunder, could have been something else. A gasp cut short. The robe whispering against tile. Silence blooming where sound had lived.

When the world righted itself, Melody found she was kneeling. The storm filled the space that voices had left behind. The room smelt of rain and perfume and the faint ozone of an extinguished candle.

Charlotte lay very still, her hair fanned across the floor like spilled light against a dark and violent plume of red. The robe had loosened, one shoulder bare, human in a way that felt indecent only because it reminded Melody what bodies were meant for before faith got involved. Her own hands hovered, uncertain, then moved with the instinct of someone arranging a scene for a painting rather than an inquest—straightening the fold of fabric, smoothing hair from a cheek.

She slipped the paperweight, taken from her father's office before she wrapped her hands around Leo's car keys, into the pocket of Nick's coat.

"You shouldn't have taken what was mine," she whispered. It wasn't anger now. It was benediction.

Thunder rolled again, close enough to rattle the window. She stood, light-headed, and her gaze caught on the small dish by the bedside table—the one with rings she recognised from the photographs. A thin silver bracelet lay among them, delicate, almost weightless. She lifted it. It chimed faintly against her palm, a sound too pretty for what it meant.

Outside, the storm began to move east, its roar receding over the river. The fluorescent light steadied. She slipped the bracelet into her pocket and stepped back into the corridor.

The door clicked shut behind her, a small, final sound swallowed by rain. She walked down the hallway, each footstep leaving a shallow, dark print that the linoleum quickly forgot. By the time she reached the exit, the wind had shifted and the air smelled newly washed, as though the town were already busy rewriting what it thought it knew.

Aftermath

Melody's drive home came in pieces, like a window someone was slow to uncover. The storm had wandered off toward the river, leaving the streets rinsed and shining, the sky a pale bruise along the roofs. Melody drove through what it left behind—mist lifting off asphalt, gutters whispering, branches still shaking off what they'd been made to hold.

The car's cabin smelt like rain. The wipers—no longer frantic—made an easy, ceremonial sweep, gifting her a momentary view of Reading composed and calm: clapboard porches damp, a paper lying darkened on a walk, a child's bicycle tipped politely on its side like a sleeping animal. Every time the glass cleared, it showed her face and then took it away again, her reflection flickering like a ghost auditioning for the role of a girl.

Her hands knew the road even when her mind didn't. Ninth Street to the light, left by the bakery with the window of untasted buns, slow over the dip that always gathered a shallow lake, the one place in town the sky could see itself. She had promised to come home. The promise had the weight of a stone carried in a pocket.

She laughed once—a small sound that startled her—then cried without sobbing, tears running as steadily as the wipers, not dramatic enough to change her breathing. Neither laughter nor crying improved anything. They were just weather, passing over the same landscape and calling it different.

"If love is faith," she whispered, because a creed with repetition becomes architecture, "I'm devout."

The words arranged the air inside the car. They gave the morning an altar.

She turned onto her street and slowed. The maples along the verge shook themselves like dogs who've spared themselves a river, sending small showers onto the hood. The Meyers house looked exactly as it had when she'd left: a front step with a hairline crack, a copper mailbox catching light like a shy halo, the potted fern Valerie tended as if it could be convinced to live forever. In the kitchen window, the lamp her mother always left on at night made its warm, human square.

She cut the engine. The sudden quiet felt theatrical, like the orchestra finding its rest after a long, difficult piece. Her fingers remained curled around the steering wheel for a breath too long. They had learned a new tremor in the storm and hadn't yet been told they could stop.

Inside, the house exhaled around her. The air smelt of coffee and damp and the faint sweetness of dish soap. The dog next door gave a solitary bark, as if taking attendance. Her shoes left small prints on the mat. She listened: the particular hush of a home as evening arrives—pipes arguing with heat, a drawer somewhere agreeing to open, the patient tick of a clock that didn't care who it woke.

Her feet found the stairs. Her room received her without judgement, that ordinary miracle. Nick's jacket clung when she shrugged it off—a wet skin peeling away from a body. She let it fall onto the chair. It held her shape for a moment, then collapsed.

She went to the bathroom and turned the tap before she was ready. Water rushed alive into the basin, clear and characterless. She held her hands under it and they moved as if rehearsed by someone else: palms together, fingers scrubbed, nails bullied, soap gathered and spent. The water went hotter; she went red. The smell of the soap was a white smell, a blank. It told the air there was nothing to narrate.

She didn't look for colour; she had decided that truth would be told by sensation. Heat rose into sting; sting turned into ache; ache into quiet. She scrubbed until the skin along her knuckles brightened and the creases in her palms protested with small, luminous lines. When she turned off the tap, the metal cooled under her touch with a kind of relief.

She dried her hands and then, without meaning to, did it all again. When she stepped back from the sink, the mirror showed her a girl with eyes too bright and lips too pale and hair stringing onto her shoulders like ribbons dragged through a river. The girl looked like she belonged to mourning. Melody did not trust her.

The bracelet waited where she had placed it on her desk, small and quiet as if it had always belonged to the room. Sterling, light, the delicate oval links reflective now that the lamp was on. When she lifted it, it made a faint, chiming sound against her fingernail, a sound too pretty for certainty. She felt for its catch. It opened with a domestic click. She closed it around her fingers as if testing fit, then slipped it off and crossed to her jewellery box —white wood, a satin-lined interior her mother had called *classic* when she gave it to her on her thirteenth birthday.

She opened the lid. The music mechanism inside had broken the year before—now it only sighed once and surrendered. She nested the bracelet among the small things that meant years of wanting: the choir pin, the bottle-green stud earrings she'd worn to the winter formal, a cheap ring that turned her finger a shy blue when it rained. She folded a square of tissue over the bracelet with the same care she used for her own name when she wrote it at the top of a page. Proof and keepsake, trophy and tenderness—the words could live together if she told them to.

When she closed the lid, the box gave a soft thunk. She felt the sound in her ribs.

Her hands remembered the confrontation. Her thoughts did not. She sat on the edge of the bed and stared at the floor until the wood stripes swam together. When she stood again, it wasn't because her mind had decided.

Downstairs, Valerie's voice moved through the kitchen, the same warm register she used for recipes, reminders, lullabies—those domestic tones with which women keep a world from falling apart. Leo murmured back, the slow, unhurried syllables of a man grateful for coffee. Melody walked toward them like a person learning to re-enter gravity.

"You're back," Valerie said, turning with a dishcloth in her hand and a damp wisp of hair stuck across her forehead. She smiled, relief flickering under it—another evening, another chance at ordinary. "Will you eat dinner with us tonight?"

"Yup," Melody said, because the response fit anywhere.

Valerie glanced past her at the greyed square of window. "That storm," she said, as if the sky were a guest who had overstayed its welcome. "It was something, wasn't it? I thought the maple would uproot itself and walk away."

Melody nodded. The rain had left a glaze on the world that made everything look deliberate. She began setting the table—plate, fork, spoon, the choreography of consent—and sat. Across the table, Leo took his seat. Max shuffled in, hair in heroic disarray, and sat at his place at the table with the solemnity of conducting a symphony.

Valerie slid a bowl toward Melody—hearty stew, the surface rippling with the slow dance of steam. Chunks of carrot and potato surfaced, soft as confession. "Eat," she said gently. "Please."

Melody lifted a spoon. She made it halfway to her mouth and paused, because the television above the fridge—the one they kept low in the background for weather and headlines and the murmur of other people— had changed its tone. The anchor's voice softened; the ribbon along the bottom turned the colour of warnings.

"...developing story out of Alvernia University this morning," the woman said, precise in her vowels, respectful in her distance. "Campus security confirms a female student was found unresponsive in her dormitory early today. Authorities have not yet released a name pending notification of family..."

The spoon hung in air, a small chrome moon.

Valerie made a sympathetic noise. "That's awful."

Leo set his glass down too carefully. "Kids," he said, meaning all of them, everywhere. "Someone's child."

"...no obvious signs of foul play," the anchor continued, an arrangement of words that meant less than it said. "Police are on scene. We'll bring you more as we learn it."

The shot changed: a live feed from the campus. The dorm's brick looked darker on television, the hedges glossier, the cluster of people under umbrellas disciplined by weather into a neat geometry. Yellow tape appeared and disappeared as the camera panned. Everything familiar became evidence by angle alone.

No name, Melody thought, and the thought had no edges; it was all centre.

Her heartbeat, which had been a drum and then a bell, became a metronome so steady she wanted to throw something to break it. In the reflection on the TV's glass, she caught her own face—a girl eating stew while the world rearranged itself to match something she had asked of it. The expression there was nothing, then everything: shock without surprise, sorrow without guilt, the unbearable rightness of a picture hung straight after a long time told it was crooked.

Valerie turned the volume down a notch, kindness dressed as caution. "They always say too much too soon," she said. "We don't know anything yet."

"I know," Melody said, and the words felt like the truth, just not the one her mother meant.

She lowered the spoon. The stew had cooled at the edges, a thin film glistening where the fat had risen. A piece of carrot drifted in the thick broth, the orange bleeding faintly into brown. She did not think of blood. She had promised herself she would think of weather and water and heat and prayer, so she did. She thought of the rain tracing lace against the dorm window; she thought of air heavy with eucalyptus and soap; she thought of the word mine placed in a room like a candle that had no intention of going out.

Valerie reached across the table, covered Melody's wrist with her hand. Her palm was warm—kitchen-warm, mother-warm, the warmth of a thousand gestures that required no permission. "You all right, sweetheart?"

Melody looked at her mother's fingers—no polish, a faint nick at the side of the nail where a knife had slipped, a small burn mark along the thumb from last Thanksgiving. Hands that healed as they worked. Hands that kept. She was aware, with sudden clarity, of what love looks like in daylight as opposed to chapel light.

"I'm fine," she said. This time, the word wasn't a door she locked behind her—it was a bridge she was grateful existed. *No obvious signs of foul play* echoed in her head, spiralling in dizzy, delirious relief.

Leo cleared his throat and stood, kissing the top of Melody's head in passing the way he always did. The ordinary felt like a miracle and like an insult—proof that the universe could be cruel and tender in the same breath. Max pushed his spoon through the stew and asked whether storms could make lightning strike the same place twice. Valerie said yes, and three times, and four, and as often as it wanted—that humans weren't made of magnets but of water and bone and luck. The television murmured in the corner, pretending not to watch them. Outside, the sky bruised into evening. Inside, the day pretended it hadn't already broken.

When Melody carried her bowl to the sink, she set it down too gently. The faucet sang at a modest pressure. Somewhere outside, a car alarm bleated twice and then remembered it had nothing to say. As the water ran over porcelain, she looked at her hands again, turned them palms up. The skin along the knuckles was pink and clean and new, the way healed places look for a while before they learn the colour of their neighbours.

Upstairs, in the jewellery box, the bracelet lay under tissue like a secret the box had agreed to keep. The thought of it there calmed her the way the sight of shoreline calms a swimmer who has been in open water too long.

She knew what her heart was supposed to do now—break under the weight of what she'd taken, fracture along the old lines into a girl-shaped ruin. Instead, in the quiet between newscaster sentences, something inside her settled. Not joy. Not triumph. A terrible, level peace, like a table righted after wobbling through a thousand meals.

She dried her hands and pressed her damp palms against the cool of the counter. Outside, the maple shimmered in the fading light, its leaves lifting toward dusk as if nothing had happened to them that couldn't be forgiven by simply being leaves again. A sparrow hopped stupidly heroic along the fence. Neighbours pulled their bins back from the curb, the wheels thudding hollow against cement. The news shifted to weather. Evening deepened. The night went on pretending it was just another one.

Melody went upstairs and closed her door and sat on the edge of the bed in a room that looked like anyone's. She opened the jewellery box to make sure the bracelet was still there and closed it again the way a person closes a Bible, respectful without reading. She lay back and stared at the ceiling, at the faint hairline crack that ran from corner to corner like a map of a river that had never flooded.

She thought the words she would not write: *The world looks balanced again*. The sentence held. It did not wobble. It did not beg for revision.

She folded her hands on her stomach, the way people once did in portraits when they were being immortalised, and let breath move in and out. The house listened, and—finding nothing dangerous in the sound— relaxed. The evening settled without asking permission. And somewhere on a campus not so far away, a corridor filled with the hush of unfamiliar footsteps, a door shut softly, a phone rang in a room that could not answer it.

Melody let her eyes close. The afterimage of the storm lay quiet behind her lids, all grey veils and brief white stitching, a sky doing needlework for its own satisfaction. She did not pray. Prayer belonged to the before. She did something simpler. She believed.

Part III

The Reckoning

The Warrant ~ Three Months Later

Dawn was the colour of surrender.

The storm had gone hours earlier, but Linden Avenue still glittered with its aftermath. Three marked cars angled across the street; an unmarked sedan idled at the curb. Breath turned to ghosts in the porch light.

Detective Alvarez checked the folded warrant, then nodded to Pritchard. They took the steps in three quick beats. Alvarez knocked—firm, even, three times.

Inside, Valerie was already awake. The kitchen lamp burned a soft gold over ribbon tails and flour dust; cinnamon hung in the air like a memory that refused to go. The knock didn't startle so much as land—authoritative, unavoidable. She opened the door.

Two plainclothes detectives in front—woman left, man right—flanked by three uniformed officers; a fourth figure watched the walkway with a camera cradled to their chest. The cold made everything sharper.

"Mrs. Meyers," Alvarez said, level and calm. She held out the papers. "We have a warrant for the arrest of Melody Meyers."

Valerie blinked once. "It's her birthday."

Pritchard's voice was gentle. "We'll make this as straightforward as possible."

They stepped inside. Wet soles marked the tile in faint ovals. From the hall, Leo appeared, belt half-laced, taking in uniforms, his wife's shoulders, the shape of his son on the stairs.

"We can't discuss details," Alvarez said, reading the warrant's essentials—judge signed, date, probable cause—with a cadence that changed the room. "You can contact an attorney. Her rights will be protected."

Upstairs, a light clicked on. Max froze at the banister. Valerie moved first—bare feet, automatic—because that's what mothers do when there is nothing else left to do.

Melody's door. A knock. The room opening on coconut shampoo, spearmint gum, a string of fairy lights, the constellation of pinned Polaroids.

"Melody," Valerie said, ordinary on purpose. "Baby, wake up."

The detectives stayed visible but back. A female uniformed officer—compact, kind-eyed—took the doorway. "I'll give you a minute to get dressed," she said after Alvarez advised rights, her voice soft enough not to bruise the hour.

Hoodie. Jeans. Socks. Shoes. The small armours. The cuffs were held low, discreet; the sound they made—metal kissing metal—was precise and obscene.

"Don't say anything," Valerie told her daughter, steady as a nurse's hand. "We'll get a lawyer."

"I know," Melody said, face smoothing to something that wasn't childhood anymore.

They walked the hall. Family photos slid past like a film strip—Max at three with a popsicle grin; Melody at ten with a ribbon; all four of them at Cape

May, sunburnt and laughing. The fourth stair creaked; Max flinched. Leo's hands lifted and fell, useless against this.

At the door, cold air rushed in. No sirens. No spectacle. Just the work of it.

"You can follow to the station," Alvarez said, arranging the words like fragile things. "Drive safe."

Outside, the unmarked sedan's door thunked shut, personal in the way a finality can be. Engines rolled away with sleepy caution. Linden Avenue went back to being a street.

Inside, the kitchen lamp still glowed over the remains of celebration: cooling cinnamon buns, ribbon trimmings, and the Happy Sweet 16, Melody! banner listing on one loosened pushpin. Valerie's phone was already in her hand. She dialled. Voicemail. Dialled again.

Leo stood at the window, watching tail-lights thin to mist. In the doorway, Max made the small shape of a question mark.

"What do we do?" Leo asked, voice sanded down.

Valerie set the phone on the counter, found the keys, and steadied herself on the edge of the island the way you steady a measuring cup to read the meniscus.

"We go," she said.

The house breathed. The lamp hummed. The banner moved a little in the furnace's sigh—like a chest rising, falling, insisting on ordinary air.

The Trial Machine

The interview room wasn't a room so much as a container: cinderblock painted the colour of compromise, fluorescent light that hummed a little high, a steel table with a seam down the middle as if it had been folded out of something larger. No clock. No window. The kind of space that convinces you time is a rumour.

Melody sat in the plastic chair with her hands in her lap, cuff marks pale bracelets at her wrists. She had been processed already—shoelaces removed, belongings inventoried, photo taken under lighting that made everyone look like a cautionary tale. A female officer had spoken in the tender monotone reserved for teenagers and grief. Then the door had closed and the room had resumed its hum.

It opened again for the lawyers.

Daniel Kessler came in first—fifty, trim, a suit the exact navy of authority. He held a thin leather folio, the kind that had been to a hundred rooms like this and learned not to pick up the air they carried. Behind him: Graham Ellis, twenty-five, jacket a half-inch too narrow in the shoulders, hair that refused to obey gel, a messenger bag slung cross-body in a way that advertised both diligence and inexperience. His eyes moved like a novice in a museum—trying to take in everything without looking impressed.

"Ms. Meyers," Kessler said, placing the folio on the table and sitting with a practised economy. "I'm Daniel Kessler. Your parents retained me this morning." A glance to the officer at the door. "We'll need privacy." The officer nodded, stepped out, the door clicked. The hum got louder for a beat, then settled.

Graham sat, opened a yellow legal pad, uncapped a pen. "I'm Graham," he said, trying for even and landing on earnest. "I'll be assisting Mr. Kessler. First—how are you holding up?"

"Graham," Kessler said quietly, a reminder of order.

Melody looked at them like visitors to a dream—one sturdy, one bright. "I'm okay," she said. Her voice was small and brave, a bird returning to a hand.

"Good," Kessler said, as if he'd asked the question. He flattened a paper in the folio. "Before anything else, we're going to lay ground rules. What we discuss in here is privileged. You do not speak to police without me present. You do not speak to other detainees about your case. You do not use the jail phones to talk about facts—those calls are recorded. No social media. No texting from anyone's borrowed phone. If someone asks you anything about what happened, the answer is: 'I want my lawyer.' Understood?"

Melody nodded. She let her hands tremble slightly in her lap—enough to be seen, not enough to look staged. She angled her body toward the young one.

"Your parents are outside," Kessler went on. "We'll brief them after we speak with you alone. There will be a bail hearing within forty-eight hours. You have no prior record, you're a minor, strong community ties—we'll argue for release to your parents with conditions. In the meantime, you'll likely remain in juvenile holding, not general population. Do not discuss the facts of the case with anyone but us. Is any of that unclear?"

"No," Melody said. Then, softer: "Thank you."

Graham wrote *bail – JV holding* in a tidy hand and underlined it twice. He glanced up and met her eyes. He'd expected fear. He was not prepared for the combination she gave him instead: steadiness and gratitude. It lodged in his chest and made a small, unprofessional home.

Kessler slid a single sheet across the table. "Standard engagement letter. We'll have your parents sign the retainer, but this acknowledges that we represent you. If there's a conflict between what you want and what they want, we take instructions from you. Initial here and here."

Her hand shook—a visible tremor, a sympathetic storm. Graham pushed the pen toward her. She reached for it with a small apology of a smile. "I'm sorry," she whispered. "I'm scared."

"It's okay," Graham said quickly.

When she'd initialled, Kessler sat back. "Now." He steepled his fingers, a gesture that had won arguments before juries and judges and at least one obstinate prosecutor. "You've been charged with second-degree murder. The Commonwealth will present this as a felony-murder theory under our homicide statutes—intent inferred from conduct. The initial evidence they have is not insignificant." He glanced down at the folio. "Security footage shows your father's car entering the campus lot behind Alvernia dorms at 3:17 p.m. and leaving at 5:02 p.m. Your phone's location data—though imprecise, and we will challenge it—puts you within that radius for a lot of that time. There are latent prints on the rear dorm railing consistent with yours; the lab will call it a partial match. The Commonwealth will also make much of your text exchanges with Ms. Nilsson—messages obtained through a warrant served this morning. And they're saying they found a piece of jewellery in your room early this morning — a bracelet — with the victim's DNA on it. And possibly yours."

Graham watched her face as the list unfurled. He expected flinches at certain words—*prints, DNA, warrant*. Instead, she went paler in a way that looked like a lamp being turned down, not off. It made him want to move the lamp closer.

"We'll attack each of these," Kessler continued. "The car footage is grainy. The timing does not prove actus reus. The fingerprint is partial and on a common surface. The DNA is a 'cannot exclude'—that's not a match; it's an invitation to reasonable doubt. The messages—" He paused. "—we'll contextualise as teenage drama, not motive. Our posture now is simple: You are innocent. You will say nothing." He looked at her as if the sentence itself could be armour. "When we go to arraignment, you will plead not guilty. You will look at the judge when I tell you to, and you will not cry unless you cannot help it."

She nodded, eyes shining deliberately. "I don't want to cry," she said. "I'm trying to be brave."

"Brave is good," Kessler said, and Graham heard the human slip under the technician.

He cleared his throat. "Can I ask—" He saw Kessler's glance and recalibrated. "—just background, so we can prepare for bail. School, extracurriculars, any counselling, that sort of thing."

Melody folded her hands. "Honour roll. Choir soloist. I volunteer with the library summer reading program. I don't drink. I don't do drugs." She looked down, then back up with exquisite timing. "I loved someone. That's all."

Graham felt the defence write itself across his chest like a wet shirt. He imagined saying those words to a judge in his best reasonable voice. *Your Honour, this is not a killer. This is a child who loved unwisely.* He pushed the thought back where it belonged.

"Tell me about Charlotte," Kessler said, and the air in the room tightened half a degree.

Melody swallowed. The motion was controlled; the glisten in her eyes rose a millimetre. "She tutored me. She was kind to my parents." A beat. "She was older. She was…"—she searched, chose a word that performed restraint—"…gracious."

"And with Nick Halpern?" Kessler asked.

"My boyfriend," she said, letting a tremor into the word *boyfriend* as if it were hard to say without breaking. "He—" She stopped. Let the silence carry meaning. "I thought we were forever."

"Did you and Charlotte argue?" Kessler's voice stayed clinical.

"Once," Melody whispered. "I went to her room. I asked her to stop." Tears pushed to the brink and hovered there, respectful. "She said she was sorry for me." A small, embarrassed laugh that immediately scolded itself for existing. "That I was young. That I didn't understand love."

"And did you leave?"

"Yes."

"Did you ever physically touch her?"

Melody's breath changed. Graham watched her shoulders register the question the way a pond registers a dropped pebble—concentric, controlled, vanishing. She shook her head. The tremor sharpened. "No," she said softly. "I didn't hurt anyone. I just... loved too hard."

Graham's pen stopped moving. There was a gravity in her voice he couldn't dismiss as theatre. He had come into the room committed to scepticism; it slid off him like rain off the hood of a car.

Kessler didn't blink. "This is important," he said, tone neutral. "If anyone suggests self-defence, accident, anything that implies contact—we will be boxed into the Commonwealth's theory. Right now, your job is to protect your silence. Every person in your life—your parents, your friends, your teachers—will be approached for statements. The press will call. They will be kind to you and cruel about you, often in the same breath. You will not answer. You will not post online. You will not keep a diary." His eyes flicked to her hands. "Do you understand?"

"Yes." She made the word sound like a vow.

Graham couldn't help himself. "Do you have a place we can point to—somewhere you were, other than campus? A receipt, a text, a call—anything that anchors you?"

"I was upset," she said. "I went for a drive to clear my head. There was a storm."

"Alone?" Kessler asked.

"Yes."

"Where did you go?"

"I don't remember," she said, and the tear finally fell, a single, disciplined drop. "I just drove until everything felt less loud."

Kessler let the silence sit. Silence is a tool, too. "All right," he said. "Then we don't reach for an alibi that isn't there. We argue the evidence is circumstantial and contaminated. We push for bail. We force the Commonwealth to prove what they can't. Between now and arraignment, we coordinate with your parents on a media plan: no statements. If a reporter shouts your name, you keep your eyes down and your face neutral. If you must speak, you say, 'I am innocent. I trust the process.' Nothing else."

Melody nodded, then did something that would have looked cheap if anyone else had done it: she reached across the table and set her hand in the no-man's-land between them, palm up, as if offering a fragile thing to a pair of surgeons. "Thank you," she said to both of them, but her eyes found Graham. "I don't know what to do. I've never—" She stopped and let breath do the work words would ruin.

Graham hesitated a heartbeat, then turned his palm up too. He didn't touch her—Kessler's rules humming in his head—but he left his hand there, close enough to be chosen. It felt like standing near a candle and deciding whether to lean in.

"We're going to help you," he said. "We believe you."

Kessler gave him a brief, unreadable look—half warning, half calculation. To the room he said, "We'll be back within the hour with clothing and essentials. A female officer will escort you to juvenile. Do not discuss your case in transport. The cameras in the hall are not for decoration."

Melody drew in a breath, let it out with a shiver. "Will the judge believe me?" she asked, and there was a child's exactness in the question that made Graham want to invent a world that could say yes.

"The judge will believe the law," Kessler said. "Our job is to give the law reasons to treat you fairly."

She nodded, took that in, tucked it away like a lesson she intended to excel at. "I didn't kill anyone," she said, not for strategy now, but like a creed. "I just loved too hard."

Graham felt the line like contact. It settled into him with the inevitability of a song you know you'll be humming long after you've forgotten where you heard it. He wrote nothing. He only looked at her and let belief assemble itself, piece by piece, until it stood on its own legs.

Kessler gathered the folio, the pen, the precautions. He stood. "We'll see you soon," he said, and knocked for the officer.

The door opened; the hum shifted. Melody's face smoothed into a public version of itself—soft, frightened, composed. As she stood to go, her gaze brushed Graham's again. The moment was small, almost careless—two people glancing at a painting they'd both pretend not to think about later.

When the door closed, the hallway took them back into its bureaucratic weather—murmurs, fluorescent buzz, a printer coughing paper into a tray. Kessler didn't break stride. "Don't fall in love with your client, Graham," he said mildly, as if asking him to pass the salt. "The Commonwealth already has."

"I won't," Graham said, and heard how unconvincing he sounded. "She's just a kid," he added.

"Good," Kessler replied, not unkind. "Now let's make sure a judge actually has a reason to believe her."

The Case Against Her ~ Two Years Later

The courthouse had learned to hold its breath. Every day of *Commonwealth v. Melody Anne Meyers*, the corridors filled before the first gavel. Reporters gathered like parishioners, their microphones angled toward doors as if waiting for communion. By the time the bailiff called the room to order, every bench was taken, the gallery a mosaic of faces—local teachers, classmates, the curious, the furious, the uninvited faithful.

The air inside Courtroom 3A was always the same: a faint perfume of dust, coffee, and old paper. The Pennsylvania state seal watched from above the bench, gold leaf dulled by fluorescent light. The judge, Hon. Margaret Kravitz, had the calm expression of a woman allergic to spectacle. Her black robe hung with mathematical precision.

"Commonwealth ready?" she asked.

Assistant District Attorney Miriam Quade rose, navy suit crisp, voice steady. "Ready, Your Honour."

"For the defence?"

Daniel Kessler stood. "Ready."

He nodded to Melody, seated between him and Graham. She wore pale blue—the colour Kessler called *reliable innocence*. Her hair had been trimmed to shoulder length, framing a face carefully drained of artifice. She looked like a girl who would volunteer at a library. The cuff marks were gone. The myth of her goodness had been freshly laundered.

The prosecution began with the story the town already believed.

"Jealousy," Quade said to the jury, pacing slowly. "Possession. An obsession that grew until love became a weapon. The defendant, fifteen years old at the time, believed she had the right to determine who was worthy of affection—and who was not. Charlotte Nilsson became the target of that belief."

She didn't look at Melody; she looked at the jurors—the teacher, the accountant, the retiree, the man who delivered mail in Exeter Township. "This case isn't about a monster. It's about a choice." She clicked the remote. On the screen, the campus security still image: the Meyers family sedan under a storm's silver light. "She drove to the victim's dormitory that day. She left less than an hour later. In that window, a young woman was bludgeoned."

The photo dissolved to text messages projected above the jury box: *You don't deserve him.*

Another: *He's mine. Stay away.*

Quade's tone softened. "The defendant wrote these words to Ms. Nilsson three days before her death. She also wrote in her journal: *Don't blame me for what comes next.*"

The gallery stirred. Valerie's hand went to her mouth. Leo stared at the table as if counting the woodgrain would keep him conscious.

Kessler's objection rose—"Context, Your Honour"—but the judge overruled gently. "Proceed."

When Quade called the first witness, the jurors straightened.

"Ms. Dana Ferguson," she said, "please take the stand."

Charlotte's roommate was twenty-one, neatly dressed, clutching a tissue she hadn't used. Her voice was steady, but her hands betrayed tremors. "I knew Charlotte since freshman year," she said. "She was kind. Careful. She never liked drama."

Quade nodded sympathetically. "Did you observe any interactions between Charlotte and the defendant?"

"Yes. Melody would show up unannounced. Once, after nine. She'd stand in the hallway if Charlotte didn't answer. I heard her crying once—saying, 'You can't take him, he's mine.'"

"Did Charlotte seem afraid?"

A pause. "She said she felt sorry for her. That Melody was... intense."

"Did Charlotte ever mention ending the tutoring sessions?"

"She said she had to. It was getting too personal. Charlotte told Mrs. Meyers she was going home for the summer."

Quade let the silence do its work before murmuring, "Thank you."

Kessler rose for cross-examination, a study in restraint. "Ms. Ferguson, you never saw any violence, did you?"

"No."

"You never saw Melody threaten Charlotte physically?"

"No."

"You said she was crying. People cry when they're hurt, not when they're violent, correct?"

"Yes."

Kessler nodded. "No further questions."

The witness stepped down. The jury shifted—sympathy uncertain, curiosity sharpened.

Next came the evidence tech, the forensic pathologist, the security officer from Alvernia. Each spoke in the language of procedure: *partial prints, inconclusive DNA, camera timestamp variance.* Kessler dismantled each point methodically, reminding the jury of what could not be proven.

Then Quade called the witness everyone had come for.

"Nick Halpern."

He looked older than his now 20 years—pale, exhausted, guilt already tattooed behind his eyes. He avoided Melody's gaze as he took the stand. His voice was rough from sleeplessness.

"You were in a relationship with the defendant?"

"Yes."

"And you were also seeing the victim, Ms. Nilsson?"

His throat worked. "Yes."

Quade paced a few steps, the quiet of the room folding around her words. "When Ms. Nilsson ended tutoring, did the defendant react?"

"She was upset. Said Charlotte was trying to take me away."

"Did she ever make threats?"

A long silence. "She said she'd rather see me dead than gone."

The gallery gasped softly, a collective intake.

Quade stopped pacing. "Did you believe her?"

"I thought she was... emotional. I didn't think she meant it."

"Thank you, Mr. Halpern."

Kessler rose, smooth as ritual. "Mr. Halpern, you cared about Melody?"

"Yes."

"And you cared about Charlotte?"

He hesitated. "Yes."

"So your feelings were... complicated."

"Yes."

"And guilt can complicate memory, can't it?"

Nick blinked. "I don't know."

"You wanted to help Charlotte. You wanted to protect Melody. And now you're caught between them."

Nick's jaw tightened. "She didn't need protecting."

Kessler leaned in slightly. "But you do?"

"Objection," Quade said. "Argumentative."

"Sustained."

Kessler smiled faintly. "No further questions."

Nick stepped down, face ghost-white. He kept his eyes on the floor as he passed the defence table. Melody's tears had started before he reached her. They came slow, deliberate, shimmering in the light.

"He's lying," she whispered, the words small but sharp enough to carry. "He's lying!" She rose from her seat.

The courtroom rippled. The bailiff took a single step forward. Judge Kravitz raised a hand. "Order. Ms. Meyers, you will remain seated."

Melody pressed her face into her hands, shoulders shaking. Every sob sounded like it might break her in half. Even the prosecutor's expression softened for a heartbeat before hardening again.

Kessler leaned in. "Enough," he murmured, low but firm. "Don't give them spectacle."

She shook her head, voice muffled. "He's lying."

Across the table, Graham reached under the surface and, without thinking, touched her hand. Just once. Her fingers tightened around his, small and trembling. He told himself it was mercy. He told himself it was control.

The jurors shifted, their collective empathy tilting. The youngest—a nurse's aide—bit her lip. The man in the third seat rubbed his temple. People liked to believe tears were truth.

Judge Kravitz called a recess. The gavel fell, two measured strikes.

Reporters surged toward the aisle, their questions a flurry of static. *Melody, did you love him? Did you kill her?* The bailiff's bark of *All rise* drowned them out.

In the defence room behind the court, Kessler removed his glasses and exhaled. "Well," he said to Graham, "half the jury wants to adopt her, half wants to burn her. That's a start."

Graham didn't answer. He was watching Melody—her damp lashes, the way she still shook, the small, grateful smile she gave him through tears that might have been real or rehearsed.

She looked at him as if she'd finally found someone who understood that love could be worship and ruin at once.

And he, despite every rule, looked back.

The Plan

Kessler's office looked different at night. The framed degrees on the wall lost their gloss. The blinds turned the streetlights into narrow, restless stripes. A half-empty bottle of bourbon kept watch by the file cabinet, a private concession to long days and impossible clients.

Graham sat at the conference table, sleeves rolled, tie askew. The fluorescent light above him flickered with the quiet patience of fatigue. The day's trial transcripts lay open in front of him—*Exhibit 47, People's Motion to Admit Prior Statements*, his own notes scrawled in the margins. He hadn't gone home since court adjourned.

When the knock came, he assumed it was Kessler returning for his briefcase.

It wasn't.

Melody stood in the doorway in the same blue coat she'd worn to court. It dwarfed her, making her look both younger and more deliberate. The ankle monitor blinked faintly beneath the hem of her jeans, its quiet pulse a reminder that freedom came with conditions. Outside, a probation officer waited in the car, giving them exactly fifteen minutes. She gave him a small nod; he pretended not to notice the unspoken request for privacy.

"Melody, what are you doing here?" Graham said, standing quickly, guilt blooming like heat.

"They let me see my lawyers," she said. "You're my lawyer."

"Technically," he corrected, "Mr. Kessler—"

She smiled faintly. "Technically."

She walked in, movements slow, almost reverent, and sat across from him. For a moment, neither spoke. The hum of the city filled the silence—a siren blocks away, tires whispering on wet pavement, the world busying itself with easier sins.

"They'll convict me," she said finally. It wasn't a question.

Graham ran a hand through his hair. "The prosecution's case isn't airtight. It's—"

"Believable," she finished for him. "That's what matters. Believable beats true."

He looked at her then—the steady eyes, the unflinching calm of someone who'd already rehearsed her verdict. "You didn't kill her."

Her smile returned, smaller this time, almost kind. "You believe that?"

"I do."

"Why?"

He hesitated. Because the alternative meant the world was uglier than he could stand. Because every time she spoke, she made guilt sound like poetry. Because he wanted to be right about something.

"Because you don't sound like someone who could," he said.

She leaned forward, her voice barely a breath. "Then help me prove it."

The words slid across the table like devotion and a dare in the same breath.

He stared. "You're talking about evidence. Evidence doesn't appear, Melody."

"Doesn't it?" Her tone was soft, almost academic. "What do you think the Commonwealth does when they can't find what they want? They tell a better story. They use the pieces that fit. I'm just asking you to tell ours."

He should have said no. He should have told her the law was a system, not a story. Instead he heard himself say, "What kind of help?"

She took something from her pocket—a folded scrap of paper, the kind officers give detainees to jot contact numbers. She slid it to him. Written in tiny block letters: *Alvernia Campus Security -Media Tips Line*.

"They take anonymous tips," she said. "If someone called and said they saw Charlotte arguing with someone else that night—someone taller, someone wearing Nick's jacket—it would make sense, wouldn't it?"

He shook his head. "That's not—Melody, that's tampering."

"It's context," she said. "You said it yourself. Believable beats true."

He looked at the scrap again. His stomach turned. "What happens when they investigate and don't find anyone?"

"They will," she said. "Because we'll give them something to find."

Her gaze didn't waver. It didn't need to. "Nick's jacket. They'll find it. It will have blood on it."

"How?"

She tilted her head. She didn't answer. "If they found something they didn't know they were looking for-something that points to him-it would raise doubt. That's all we need."

"Melody—"

"I don't want to hurt anyone," she interrupted, and the tremor in her voice was perfect. "I just want my life back."

He stood, paced to the window, looked down at the rain-spattered glass. His reflection looked older than it had that morning. "You're asking me to risk everything."

"I'm asking you to keep faith."

The phrase hung there like incense—suffocating, sweet.

*   *   *   *   *

It started with small trespasses.

An email chain from campus security to the district attorney's office— routine coordination. Graham saw it in discovery, forwarded for administrative review. The server login required a two-factor code, easily circumvented with the right delay between requests. He told himself he was checking for Brady material—exculpatory evidence the prosecution hadn't disclosed. He told himself it was diligence.

The tip came next. The voicemail system for media inquiries didn't require authentication, only a voice. Melody recorded it in a whisper over the jail's phone line, then played it back for him in the visitation room, her tone pitched to anonymity.

Saw the girl fighting with a guy in a navy jacket near the dorm lot. Blonde. He shoved her. I think he drove off in a blue Honda. I saw him throw something out the window. It looked like the jacket. Don't want to get involved.

Blue Honda. Nick's car. Navy jacket. Nick's jacket.

The next morning, Graham found the bracelet. It lay in a plastic evidence bag marked *DET EX-9: Personal Effects - M. Meyers.* The tag indicated non-probative, cleared for release to property. No one would notice if one item took the long way home. He returned it to Melody.

He hated how steady his hands were as he worked the seal open. The silver glimmered under the fluorescent light. He could still smell the faint antiseptic of the evidence room.

*   *   *   *   *

The news broke two days later: NEW EVIDENCE RAISES QUESTIONS IN MEYERS CASE

A campus maintenance worker, responding to an anonymous tip, had located a jacket belonging to Nicholas Halpern, seen the night of Charlotte Nilsson's murder, with the victim's blood on it. Investigators were re-examining prior witness statements. The Commonwealth declined comment pending further inquiry.

Kessler slammed the newspaper onto his desk. "What the hell is this?"

Graham looked at the print, at the headline already curling under the weight of its own ink. "Reasonable doubt," he said quietly.

Kessler stared at him for a long time. "Don't get creative, Ellis. The law doesn't thank artists."

Graham didn't answer. Outside the window, the rain had started again, gentle now, like someone blessing the city with restraint.

Later, just before court, Melody's eyes were bright with something close to wonder. She reached out and touched his fingers.

"You did it," she whispered.

He shook his head. "You did."

She smiled—a faint, private curve of her lips. "If love is faith," she said, the words tasting like prophecy, "then we're both devout."

The Verdict

The last day of trial began the way ordinary mornings do—sunlight pale and polite over the courthouse lawn, a line of reporters with coffee cups steaming into the cold.

Reading had been living with this case for months now; it had become part of the town's bloodstream, a slow, steady pulse of speculation.
Inside Courtroom 3A, the air carried that particular silence that only verdict days have: half reverence, half hunger.

Melody sat at the defence table between Kessler and Graham, her posture perfect, hands folded neatly in her lap. Her blue suit had been replaced with cream, the colour Kessler said read as hope. The pearl bracelet she wore—borrowed from her mother, not the other one—caught the light each time she turned her wrist.

The Commonwealth's table looked exhausted. Miriam Quade flipped through her closing notes, their corners soft from use. The new evidence —Nick's arrest two weeks earlier—had shifted the trial's gravity. The newly recovered jacket, the anonymous tip, the emails suggesting his contact with Charlotte hours after her death—it all told a new story. A story that wasn't true, but looked like one.

"Commonwealth v. Meyers, docket number 2025–2719," the bailiff announced, his voice thin against the wood-paneled room. "All rise."
The jury filed in. Twelve people who had once been strangers and were now architects of a girl's future. The foreman carried the verdict form folded in his hand, paper trembling slightly.

Judge Kravitz looked down from the bench, composed as stone. "Has the jury reached a verdict?"

"We have, Your Honour."

The clerk stepped forward, received the paper, unfolded it with bureaucratic care. The room inhaled and forgot how to exhale.

"On the charge of Murder in the Second Degree," the clerk read, "we, the jury, find the defendant, Melody Anne Meyers—"

A pause, as deliberate as punctuation.

"—not guilty."

For a moment, the words didn't register. They hung there, suspended, fragile as glass. Then the air rushed back in.

Valerie's sob broke the silence first. She covered her mouth, shoulders shaking. Leo put an arm around her, eyes wet, jaw tight.

Kessler exhaled through his nose, the exact expression of a man who'd expected victory and still couldn't quite believe in it.

Graham's pen rolled off the table, clattering softly to the floor.

Melody didn't move. Her face stayed perfectly still. Then—like sunlight breaking through fog—a slow, careful smile appeared. Tears followed, measured, convincing.

Judge Kravitz thanked the jurors, dismissed them with the usual instructions about confidentiality. Reporters in the back rows were already standing, phones lifted, the future streaming in real time.

When the gavel fell, it sounded like absolution.

The courthouse steps gleamed under late afternoon sun. The press had grown since morning, a wall of microphones and questions. The blue-and-white Reading Chronicle van idled at the curb, its camera mounted like an accusation.

Melody stepped into the light, flanked by Kessler and Graham. Valerie and Leo followed close behind, their relief visible, their exhaustion holy. The crowd erupted—shutters clicking, voices overlapping.

"Melody! Do you have anything to say?"

She paused, blinked against the brightness, tilted her chin toward the sky as though listening to something only she could hear.

"I believe in love," she said clearly, her voice soft but certain. "And I believe in forgiveness."

The words landed like a benediction.

A reporter called out, "Who do you forgive, Melody?"

She only smiled—beatific, unreadable—and let the question hang.

Valerie broke then, pulling her daughter into her arms. "You're free," she whispered. "It's over."

Leo joined them, his hand trembling on Melody's back. Cameras flashed, catching the three of them in tableau: mother, father, daughter, redemption.

Kessler adjusted his tie, expression satisfied. To him, this was justice by design—reasonable doubt weaponized into mercy. He gave a short statement to the press, all gratitude and professionalism, his voice cutting clean through the noise.

Graham stood a few steps behind, watching her. The crowd's roar muted in his ears until there was only the sight of her face—the calm, the glow, the terrible peace of it. She looked like someone who had come through fire and been made pure by it.

For a moment, he believed his own invention. He saw not the girl who'd whispered to him, not the hand that had guided his into sin, but something transcendent: a girl who had loved too hard and survived the punishment.

The flashbulbs burned white halos around her. In the photographs printed the next morning, she would look sainted.

Graham didn't notice Kessler watching him, or the way the detective from the DA's office lingered across the street, smoking and staring as though the story had left too many edges unresolved.

He only saw Melody turning toward him, eyes clear, the faintest curl of a smile forming—the kind that said she already knew he'd follow her anywhere.

Part IV
The Aftermath

The Whisper Campaign

The trial ended, but the story didn't. It only changed narrators.

Reading was a town that loved its myths tidy. The papers ran her photograph again the following week—Melody on the courthouse steps, eyes lifted, a half-smile poised between relief and revelation. Underneath, the caption: The Girl Who Believed in Love. The image did what the verdict could not. It split the town cleanly down the middle.

At the diner off Penn Street, people said Nick Halpern had it coming. At the grocery store, they whispered that girls like Melody were born knowing how to lie. In the high school hallways, her name became shorthand for obsession, or resilience, depending on who said it. The truth was irrelevant; the story was what mattered. It made people feel safer to choose a side.

For Melody, the noise outside was oxygen. Sympathy arrived in casseroles, in letters written in looping cursive, in the small, trembling hands of mothers who wanted to believe the world could still forgive their children anything. She learned how to tilt her head just so when someone said, You poor thing. She learned that grief and grace wore the same dress if you stood in the right light.

At night, the house filled with the hush of gratitude—Valerie murmuring thanks to neighbours, Leo talking about moving somewhere quieter, Max learning not to mention Charlotte's name. On the news, Nick stood in court in a borrowed suit while the judge said twenty to forty years as if numbers could measure grief. Melody watched it once, face unreadable, then asked her mother to change the channel.

She didn't need to see it. She had already memorised the shape of victory.

Graham visited once a week at first, then more often. It began under the pretext of paperwork—follow-ups, appeals, routine post-trial housekeeping—but the conversations wandered.

Kessler teased him for caring too much. "She's a client, Ellis. Not a cause."

Graham didn't correct him. He already knew the difference was academic.

The first time he saw her alone after the verdict, it was in the Kessler office conference room. She'd come with her parents to sign post-release forms; they'd stepped out to take a call. Melody lingered by the window, fingers tracing the faint condensation on the glass.

"They still look at me like I might break," she said.

"You won," he replied. "You're free."

She turned, smiling slightly. "Freedom's a trick word. People use it when they want to stop thinking."

He wasn't sure how to answer that. Her gaze didn't leave him. It was too steady, too knowing. The silence stretched until she added, almost gently, "You look tired."

He laughed, nervous, too loud. "It's been a long journey."

"You did everything for me," she said, and it wasn't gratitude so much as recognition. "Everyone else, I could see the skepticism on their faces. You believed."

She stepped closer. The air between them shifted. He felt it in the nerves behind his eyes—the faint, electric warning of being seen too clearly.

"You shouldn't be here after hours," he said quietly, closing the door behind him.

"I could say the same about you," she murmured.

He hesitated. "The building locks at ten."

"I know." She rose from the chair, slow, deliberate. "You keep your key in your briefcase."

The air between them shifted. He felt it behind his eyes—the faint, electric warning of being seen too clearly.

"You think I'm innocent," she said, stepping closer, her perfume threading through the room—something floral, faintly sweet, impossible to name. "So you have to keep proving it. Otherwise you'd have to ask what kind of man risks everything for a lie."

The words slid beneath his skin like a current. "Melody—"

She tilted her face up, small and certain. "Don't worry," she whispered. "I won't tell anyone what kind of man you are."

He should have stepped back. Instead, he caught her wrist—an instinct, a plea, a surrender—and in the stillness that followed, she kissed him first.

It was soft, then not. A collision disguised as permission.

*   *   *   *   *

The whispers spread faster than the truth ever had.

People said Graham Ellis had ruined his career for her.

They said she sent him letters in handwriting neat enough to pass for scripture.

They said she visited him at his apartment on the west side, that the lights stayed on until dawn.

None of it could be proven, but all of it was true.

When Kessler confronted him one morning—news clipping in hand, jaw tight—Graham didn't deny it. "She's 18," he said weakly.

Kessler's look was weary, not angry. "No," he said. "She's a lesson. And you're about to fail it."

But Graham had already stopped believing in lessons. He'd chosen faith instead.

*   *   *   *   *

The next time Melody saw him, it was at the quiet café—the one where no one would recognise her except the waitress who kept their secrets for tips. She wore a soft grey sweater and light makeup. Her hair caught the light the way sincerity does.

"They're still talking," he said.

"Let them," she said. "It's what people do when they don't understand miracles." She reached across the table and touched his wrist, her feet brushing his beneath it.

He watched her stir sugar into her coffee—slow, deliberate, ritualistic. The silver bracelet caught the light, a small, shining reminder of everything he'd already risked to believe her.

"Sometimes," she said, not looking up, "I think people only ever fall in love with what they've saved. Doesn't it make you feel holy?"

He should have walked away. Instead, he nodded.

She smiled, slow and devastating. "Good," she said. "Then don't ever stop."

He paid the bill without speaking. When they stepped outside, the rain was still falling—fine, silver, impossible to stay dry in. They didn't bother trying. The streetlamps blurred in the mist, each one a small confession.

She took his hand. It wasn't coy or secret; it was claiming. He let her lead him through the quiet blocks to his building, the sound of their footsteps soft as breath.

In the elevator, she leaned her head against his shoulder. He could smell the rain in her hair, the faint trace of coffee and something sweeter. The floor numbers climbed.

By the time they reached his door, the city had gone silent. She turned to him, eyes luminous and certain. "Don't blame me," she whispered. "Love has a way of making me crazy."

The kiss that followed was the slow unraveling of restraint—the kind that feels like worship more than want. The lights stayed low, the storm doing all the talking.

When morning came, the world was rinsed clean again, and the air still smelled faintly of rain and surrender.

The Pattern

The years didn't pass so much as dissolve, leaving behind the outline of a woman who was always becoming someone new.

Reading receded into myth—first a place, then a story, then a caution told in low voices. The verdict faded from the papers, the courthouse grew ivy, and people forgot which version of the truth they had believed.

But Melody never forgot.

She learned that leaving was easier if you did it before anyone asked you to stay. She changed her hair to something softer, lighter, something that didn't remind her of a girl who'd once stood on courthouse steps promising forgiveness. The first city took her like a tide: Philadelphia, a year of brick row houses and train whistles, the air always smelling faintly of iron and rain.

She took an apartment above a florist. The owner, an older woman with the kind of voice that could calm storms, let her water the hydrangeas on the front stoop each morning. "You've got a gentle way," the woman said once. Melody smiled and didn't correct her.

At night, she walked through Rittenhouse Square, watching couples in the yellow pools of lamplight. Their laughter came in bursts—bright, careless things she could almost touch. Sometimes she imagined walking up to them, saying her name just to see if it meant anything anymore.

It never did.

She met her first husband in that city. Caleb Hines. Wealthy, magnetic, the kind of man who filled a room by not needing to. She found him at a gallery opening—photographs of strangers caught mid-confession—he told her she looked like she belonged inside the frame. He said she was haunting.

She said she'd been told that before.

He loved her in the way men love the unknowable: with awe, and with the arrogance of thinking awe might one day translate into ownership. He bought her dresses the colour of smoke, flew her to New Orleans for weekends, whispered that she was *his calm*.

When he died—fell, jumped, slipped; no one could decide—she wept in front of everyone who needed her to. Her grief was flawless, her voice breaking in places that sounded rehearsed only if you already knew the melody.

The newspapers ran a photograph of her leaving the memorial. Head bowed. Lips parted as if in prayer. A caption that called her "a figure of composure amid tragedy."

It wasn't the first time they'd written that sentence. It was far from the last.

*   *   *   *   *

Baltimore was next. A city of brick and harbour light. Melody said she chose it for the water, but really she chose it because no one there had heard of her. She rented a studio with tall windows and painted the walls white so the daylight would stay longer.

Daniel Leighton arrived by accident—an architect consulting on her building's restoration. He had the kind of confidence that came from being good at things that could collapse if you weren't. He liked symmetry. He liked Melody's young face because it made him feel safe.

He told his colleagues she was unlike anyone he'd met. He told her she made the world quieter. She smiled, because quiet was her native tongue.

Their wedding was small: lilies, champagne, a band that played too softly. Her dress wasn't white but something close enough that no one noticed.

When his car went off the bridge in the rain six months later, she watched the news without expression. They said it was hydroplaning, that he hadn't been wearing a seatbelt. The coroner used the word *accident* three times.

At the funeral, people cried harder because she didn't.

She wore black for weeks, then grey. She didn't attend the trial because it never happened.

*   *   *   *   *

After that, time blurred. Chicago for a year—wind biting through the seams of her coat. Then Portland, where she ran a photography studio that only ever shot in black and white. A brief stint in Austin, where she went by Mel Hart.

Each life folded into the next, the edges softening until only she could tell where one ended and another began. She collected new last names the way some people collected postcards—proof of places she'd once survived.

In every city, she rented near water: rivers, lakes, harbours. She liked reflections—how they told the truth differently.

And always, the rumours came.

A co-worker who flirted too freely stopped showing up to work. A woman at the gym who'd joked about "stealing her husband" moved away abruptly and was never seen again. A neighbour's wife packed a single suitcase and was never seen again.

The police looked, but not too hard. Melody was gracious when they came to ask. She made coffee, offered tissues, thanked them for caring. Her eyes—those calm, unblinking eyes—made every suspicion sound impolite.

They left believing she was kind. And believing she was innocent.

*   *   *   *   *

She aged beautifully, though age didn't touch her much. Lines appeared and vanished, her voice deepened slightly, her grief changed flavour but not tone. The world liked women like that—ones who carried tragedy elegantly.

The bracelet was the only thing that stayed constant. Always silver, always on her wrist. When people asked, she said it was sentimental. No one ever asked whose it was.

At night, she dreamed of Reading. Of rain against glass. Of a boy with ink-stained fingers saying her name like a secret. She would wake with her heart steady and her hands cool.

By morning, she had become whoever the day required.

Some said she was unlucky in love. Some said she was cursed. Some whispered that she was the curse itself.

But the truth, if you could call it that, was simpler: Melody had learned the difference between guilt and destiny. One asked to be forgiven; the other expected worship.

And wherever she went, people gave her both.

She didn't need to run anymore. Only to arrive.

And when the cameras found her again—because they always did—she would look into the lens with that same soft expression, eyes luminous, mouth slightly parted, as if she'd been caught mid-prayer.

Forgiveness suited her.

It always had.

Graham's Fate

Winter had come back to Pennsylvania the way guilt does—quietly, uninvited, with a beauty that almost excused it. The maples along the interstate were bare, their branches black etchings against a sky the colour of paper left out in the rain.

Graham Ellis hadn't seen Reading in more than a decade. When the bus crested the hill and the town appeared—its smokestacks, its small, loyal skyline—his stomach tightened, as if his body recognised a sin before his mind did.

He still wore the same coat from those years at Kessler's firm, though the fabric had thinned at the elbows and smelled faintly of damp. His face had changed: older, yes, but also stripped down, all the bright, eager faith gone. The eyes were the same. They carried the weight of having looked at her too long.

He told himself he had come to confess. To atone. To stop pretending that the trial had been justice rather than theatre. He had documents—old emails, copies of evidence logs, fragments of the truth no one else had kept. He'd spent years thinking about that bracelet Melody had worn on her wrist for as long as he had known her, of the jacket she knew the location of and the blood on it's sleeve and inside it's pocket, about the anonymous tip that had started the avalanche.

The story had eaten him alive, piece by piece, until the only way to stop it was to tell it.

He called her first. A number she'd shared with him via email—she always kept him close, even when she was far. When her voice answered, soft and familiar, the years fell away like paint in rain.

"Graham," she said, using his name like a benediction. "I wondered when you'd find me again."

Her voice was calm. Her calm had always been the most dangerous thing about her.

"I know what we did," he said. "I can't keep it quiet anymore."

A pause. Then, gentle: "Then don't."

"I'm coming to see you."

"I'll make tea," she said. "You still take it with sugar?"

*   *   *   *   *

She lived north of the city now, in a house that overlooked the river. It was the kind of place people called peaceful because they didn't know how to read silence. The garden was disciplined, the windows immaculate.

When she opened the door, she looked almost the same. A little older, perhaps, but in the way marble ages—more defined, more certain of what it's meant to be. She smiled, and the smile was memory.

"Come in," she said.

Inside, the air smelled faintly of jasmine and rain. He thought of the courtroom, the way she had looked at him when the verdict was read—

calm, glowing, forgiven.

They sat at the kitchen table. She poured tea. His hands shook when he lifted the cup.

"I shouldn't have done it," he said. "The bracelet. The jacket. I thought I was saving you."

"You were," she said.

"I wasn't." He laughed once, bitterly. "You didn't need saving."

She tilted her head. "Everyone does, Graham."

She reached across the table and brushed at a greying lock of his hair. Graham tilted his face into her palm, his lips brushing against her soft skin.

When she pulled her hand away, his eyes opened, and for him, it felt like they truly opened.

"How did you know about the jacket?" he asked—the question he'd wanted to ask ten years ago.

Melody smiled and rose from the table, crossing to her desk with practiced elegance. She lifted a sphere of glass—a paperweight—and rolled it between her palms.

"You killed her?" Graham said. "With that?" He stayed calm, took another sip from his mug.

He looked at her then and saw it—the same quiet conviction that had once passed for faith. The same darkness dressed in devotion.

"I've read about you over the years," he began. "You killed them," he said. "All of them."

She didn't deny it. She only smiled. "You still believe in confessions. I've always admired that about you."

He pushed back from the table. "I'm going to the police."

"You won't," she said softly, as the tremor began in his hands. The cup tipped, spilling lemon and ginger across the table. The faint scent of roots and flowers rose with the steam—aconite, bitter and beautiful.

She strode back toward him and caught his weight as his knees gave way. She lowered him gently, cradling his head, and pressed a kiss to his temple.

*　　*　　*　　*　　*

Two weeks later, hikers found what the snow hadn't finished covering—a human shape beneath the pines in Berks County woodland. The papers said his name like it was a footnote: *Former defence associate found deceased; no foul play suspected.*

The news said he'd gone missing. His car was discovered days earlier at a trailhead north of the city. The coroner cited heart failure—sudden, unpreventable, a tragedy of timing. No one looked closer. The story didn't need a second life.

Valerie read the article at her kitchen table and thought of a long-ago morning and a birthday banner drooping over cold cinnamon rolls. She folded the paper neatly, as if that might keep the world from reopening old wounds.

Across the state, Melody stood by her window, watching the river move under its crust of ice. The tea kettle whistled faintly behind her. She didn't turn.

The world outside was still, patient, forgiven.

She raised her wrist, admiring the bracelet—silver, delicate, beautiful. It caught the light just so.

When she smiled, it was small and perfect.

She'd always been good at endings.

Epilogue ~ The Devil Your Loved

The radiator in Nick Halpern's apartment made a small ticking sound, like someone trying to remember a melody one note at a time. Outside, February leaned its weight against the glass, a cheap rental window with a frame painted too many times to close properly. The building was the kind that pretends to be warmer than it is: hallway carpet thinning in the centre, a faint smell of boiled cabbage and bleach, someone's laundry strung on a line just visible from the fire escape. Tenants had planted plastic geraniums in the front planter and never took them in, so even under frost there were flowers.

He was thirty. Ten years had passed and most of them had been served somewhere else. He'd learned how to sleep with the lights on. He'd learned to fold things small. He'd learned what it felt like to be looked at by people who had already decided what you were. The state had called his years "time served" with a phrase that made them sound like a meal pushed across a counter. Paroled for good behaviour, they'd said, as if goodness were a posture you could practise in a mirror until you did it convincingly enough to be believed.

The parole officer had been kind in the bureaucratic way, offering pamphlets with glossy covers full of dead verbs: *re-entry, resources, community partners*. Nick kept the stack in a drawer with the lid to a takeout container and a coil of extra wire. He worked nights at a warehouse off the highway, an ocean of boxes that smelled like cardboard and old rain. The pay wasn't terrible. The foreman didn't ask questions. The other guys kept a respectful distance, the way you do when a story has walked into the room and pretends not to be one.

Sometimes, between pallets, he'd hum to himself—the way you check if a voice still belongs to you. He didn't sing much. The songs stuck in his throat and turned to grit.

He hadn't put anything on the walls. It wasn't that he'd decided not to—he just hadn't decided to. There's a difference, and it matters. Still, he'd lined the window with small objects, anchors against the blankness: a river stone from Berks County he'd carried in his pocket the day he was sentenced; a stub of a pencil; a tin soldier, the kind kids buy at antique markets because someone once told them it had been loved; a Polaroid from a decade ago, so overexposed the faces—his and Melody's—had burned into pure light. When the wind slipped past the gasket and into the room, the pencil rolled and tapped against the glass, a soft reminder that something was still moving.

The news hummed low on the television because silence had begun to creak too loudly in his ears. Most nights it was weather, repeat traffic, a sports anchor grateful for something to narrate. He'd learned to listen without listening, the way he'd learned to eat without taste. The TV threw a pale light across the room that made everything look haunted. He didn't mind. Haunted felt honest.

That evening, he'd boiled pasta on the two-burner and eaten it standing at the sink, the radio in the next apartment playing a love song so sweet it made his teeth ache. Someone in 3B laughed at a joke Nick tried to imagine. He washed and dried the bowl with a dish towel clean enough to be a wish, then took the chair by the TV, the one with a spring that announced itself whenever he shifted. He kept the remote in his hand but never changed the channel—habit from years when you didn't control what came next.

The crawl at the bottom of the screen changed colour. Red, then white text. BREAKING NEWS. He thought, automatically, of snow closings, a pile-up on the interstate, a late-night city council scandal that would matter to no one in the morning. The anchor's voice changed its register—smooth, serious, a tone calibrated for catastrophe.

"In breaking news tonight," she said, and the room narrowed around the words, "convicted murderer Melody Meyers, twenty-eight, has been arrested in connection with the death of her husband, Julian Reeves, thirty-four."

His whole body went still. It wasn't shock—shock belongs to people who haven't practised this. It was that hard quiet you get when a sound comes from a memory you've kept underwater and it surfaces fully formed and breathing.

"Police believe she may also be connected to the deaths of at least eleven men and women across multiple states," the anchor continued.

The photo they used first was not new. It was the courthouse-steps one—cream suit, pearls, eyes lifted. He'd seen it enough times that the pixels were their own kind of prayer. Then the image changed. The booking photo was clean, almost elegant: flat light, hair pulled back, the soft shadow of the chain at her wrists just visible at the bottom edge. Older. Still beautiful. Eyes hollow not like caves, but like instruments that had been played too long.

Nick leaned forward. The radiator ticked once, twice, then held its breath. The anchor desk gleamed like a surgical tray. A second voice—someone on scene—came in with the field report: sirens, a house behind yellow tape, neighbours using words like quiet and polite, lights from a dozen stations turning wet pavement into a string of cheap jewels.

On the split screen, the caption settled in as if reluctant to name her: Meyers Arrested.

The reporter's voice steadied. "Authorities say the investigation is ongoing but believe this may be part of a larger pattern spanning more than a decade. They describe Meyers as highly intelligent, socially adept, and capable of extraordinary deception."

He didn't move. The sound kept going, but the world had already gone quiet.

He didn't change the channel. The word *arrested* sat on the screen like a prayer he hadn't meant to say aloud. It wasn't relief; it was recognition.

The broadcast ended. The room filled itself with quiet. The radiator ticked again, the sound of an old heart testing its faith.

He sat until the television cooled, thinking of the way she had once laughed when he told her that love was supposed to make people better. He understood now that she had taken the word *supposed* as permission.

He remembered her voice—soft, insistent, certain that devotion could be a weapon if you held it right. He remembered the feel of her name in his mouth and how it had always tasted a little like surrender.

He still believed her. That was the worst part. He believed every word she'd ever said about love. He had mistaken its direction, that was all. He had thought love was something that saved you. He had never considered that it might be something that chose you and refused to let go.

The radiator sighed. Outside, a siren blurred into distance.

He whispered, "I should have understood," and the words felt like confession.

*   *   *   *   *

Interrogation rooms never change. Their walls learn patience. Their ceilings hold their breath. The hum is constant; the table knows its job.

Melody sat with her wrists cuffed, the metal bright against her skin. Her hair was pulled back, deliberate, not ashamed.

Detective Alvarez—older now, steady in the way loss makes people steady—sat opposite her. She set a file on the table but didn't open it. A young partner waited by the door, pretending not to listen.

"Ms. Meyers," Alvarez said. "Your counsel is on the way. We'll wait."

Melody smiled. Not sweetly. Accurately. "Waiting's just another form of attention, Detective."

Alvarez didn't answer. Silence was the room's native tongue.

"You know why you're here," she said at last.

"The late Mr. Reeves," Melody replied, "and the others."

Alvarez nodded once. "The others."

"You're looking for closure," Melody said. "It's such a pretty word for an ending no one believes in."

The door opened. The lawyer entered—new suit, new scent, practiced detachment. "Detective," he said, "we're not speaking tonight."

"I know," Alvarez said. "We were just saying hello."

"Then say goodbye," he replied.

Alvarez stood. "You'll be arraigned in the morning."

Melody's smile deepened, unbothered. "You'll come back," she said. "Everyone does."

The lawyer's hand hovered at her shoulder; it landed nowhere.

As Alvarez gathered the file, the cuffs caught the light. The camera blinked its red acknowledgement.

"Detective," Melody said softly before Alvarez could leave the room, "you've been wondering if it was love."

Alvarez paused.

"It was," Melody said. "It always is."

You've Reached The End But...
The Stories Never Stop

Songs To Stories is exactly what it sounds like—short, emotionally devastating, romantically charged, and occasionally unhinged novellas inspired by the one and only Taylor Swift. Because why simply listen to a song when you can spiral into an entire fictional universe about it?

A new novella drops on the 13th of every month, so if you have commitment issues, don't worry—you don't have to wait long for your next dose of heartbreak, longing, and characters making wildly questionable life choices in the name of love.

To keep up with the latest releases, visit BrittWolfe.com —or don't, and risk missing out while the rest of us are already crying over the next one. Your call.

See you at the next emotional wreckage.

About The Author
Britt Wolfe

Britt Wolfe was born in Fort McMurray, Alberta, and now lives in Calgary, where she battles snow, writes stories, and cries over Taylor Swift lyrics like the proud elder Swiftie she is. She loves being part of a fan base that's as passionate as it is melodramatic.

She's married to a smoking hot Australian (her words, but also probably everyone else's), and together they parent two fur-babies: Sophie, the most perfect husky in the universe, and Lena, a mischievous cat who keeps them on their toes—and their furniture in shreds.

When Britt's not writing or re-listening to "All Too Well (10 Minute Version)," she's indulging her love for reading, potatoes in all forms, and the colour green. She's also a huge fan of polar bears, tigers, red pandas, otters, Nile crocodiles, and—because they're underrated—donkeys.

Her life is full of love, laughter, and just enough chaos to keep things interesting.

 @the.banality.of.britt

 BrittWolfe.com

www.ingramcontent.com/pod-product-compliance
Lightning Source LLC
Chambersburg PA
CBHW082226140626
46556CB00020B/3345